THE BOXING DAY FRAUD

BY
ROY ADAMS

Published by
Roy Adams

Acknowledgments

The Midland Hotel Manchester for showing me their fine hotel; Bill and Don; for being first readers, David and Mark my unpaid editor and proofreaders who unstintingly gave their time and expertise

Cover design by Ann Grigoriu

Security Note

The fraud techniques detailed in these books were current at the time of the events described. Security systems have been updated, and computers now trace everything. Do not try to emulate anything herein.

YOU WILL BE CAUGHT

Warning

This world is of organised crime, drugs and prostitution. There are explicit scenes of sex and violence with strong language throughout that some readers may find offensive, but it is the world of the criminal.

Contents

Preface:

My name is Roy Adams, and I am an Investigative Journalist. My area is mysteries and unsolved crimes, searching court records, newspaper reports, and interviewing people who were or may have been involved. Then sell the story to a newspaper or tv company, or like this write a book. It's like a giant jigsaw puzzle but you don't have all the pieces or a picture of what happened. This one started with a single piece, a rumour.

A big fraud had happened on Boxing Day 1981 to the British High Street stores. There were no court records of anyone being arrested. In fact, there were no records at all, just a large dip in the economy at the time, unsolved murders and two names, Joe and someone called 'The Professor'. It was also rumoured that the fraud was so big the authorities put a 'D' notice on the whole thing as they feared a copy-cat crime that could only be prevented by the 'Stores' changing their systems that would take years.

What was also strange was there had not been any major wars between the rival criminal gangs for about 15 years. Then suddenly in 1982 they started again with no apparent reason.

I never got all the pieces of the jigsaw, and they didn't come in the right order. This intrigued me, I wanting to know more. Then I tracked down 'Joe' to an island called St Kitts in the Caribbean.

This is his story, told by him. It fitted together with what I knew, but there are missing pieces and gaps that I have had to fill in with artistic licence, some pieces didn't seem to fit at all, that I've had to leave out. I have also been told by different people two different ways the whole thing finished.

It is you the reader who must decide which is the correct ending. Also is it a dramatization of an actual crime or if it is a complete work of fiction with events and characters described fictional and any resemblance to any event or anyone living or dead coincidental.

Roy Adams

Chapter 1

It's a hell of a day when you are told that your company is going to fail. Not today, or next week, or even next year but over the coming years your work will dry up, strangled by changing technology.

My company Read & Son had been founded by my grandfather in 1910, but my father had been the one who made the money, printing ration books and ID cards for the government during the 2nd World War. After the war we continued printing for the government plus cheques for the high street banks. I say my company but although I was the Managing Director I only had Dad's 33% shares in the company I had inherited when he died; the rest were held by father's two sisters.

My father firmly believed in 'the old school tie' insisting I had the best education sending me to Eton from where I went on to Oxford. I joined the family firm after receiving my master's degree in philosophy, politics and economics, becoming the Sales Director and then Managing Director when my father died.

Now my old school and university chums were in high office in Whitehall or Members of Parliament in the House of Commons or the House of Lords, and they called me for advice on new projects needing security documents such as ID cards and documents, or printed forms that controlled information. This I willingly did for when the government's buying agency put the jobs out for tender, they just happened to fit our machines perfectly and we won a lot of contracts.

However, the word from my friends in The Home Office was that the public purse was losing millions in fraud. The Government Think Tank on document security was recommending that paper-based transactions be phased out in favour of computer transactions as they were more secure and cheaper to process.

The banks with their credit cards had shown it could be done, and they were also determined to eliminate personal cheques completely in favour of electronic transactions to reduce fraud.

The British Government agreed with the recommendation and believed that if this policy was announced, even unofficially, the IT companies would develop the systems to fill the need. This being so they forecast that by 2000 the government machine would be paperless.

This meant the end of our company for this was what we did, it was all going to vanish; the company would be worthless. It would take at least ten years or more to get the infrastructure in place like computer terminals in the post offices, but it was going to happen. There was only one option and that was to sell while we still had something to sell so I called a shareholder's meeting.

The factory was in Belper in Derbyshire in an old cotton spinning mill; the boardroom reflected the heyday of the industry with its oak panelling and huge boardroom table before it in turn had succumbed to changing technology and cheap imports. The room was lit by a single chandelier high in the ornate ceiling; with no windows, it did little to dispel the dark and the gloom, matching my own sense of foreboding. There were four of us round that table; my two aunts plus Phillips the company secretary and me. My twin spinster aunts dressed so alike you could not tell one from another but there the similarity ended. Aunt May had dominated her younger sister all their lives, being born five minutes before her. Phillips was by far and away the oldest one present as he used to be my grandfather's secretary keeping immaculate minutes for the last sixty years and still dressed as if he was in the 1910s. No one knew how old he was, and he looked more like a pallbearer, which was probably appropriate considering my news.

Aunt May was glaring at me as if I was the devil tempting her to some awful deed. Suddenly she could hold herself no longer and with an explosive outburst said, 'Sell the company. Have you gone mad? I knew my brother was wrong leaving his shares to you. You're far too impetuous to be trusted with major decisions. Your grandfather set this company up in 1910 and I can speak on behalf of Aunt Jane and myself; we will not sit here and let you throw it away on some rumour from one of your cronies.'

'I am not saying throw it away but sell it, so you have something to live on. I can get another job, but if we don't sell now, we will end up with nothing when the factory closes.'

'You're just trying to frighten us and anyway you say it's going to be years before this happens'.

'Yes, years before it's complete but it will be a gradual process as first one item then another is converted. The government has its own factories and its common sense they will keep more work in house as items disappear. It will mean less work comes out to tender so we will be the first to be hit by the changes.'

'So go and get new work from somewhere else,' she said.

'It's not that easy. We have become highly specialised over the years, and our equipment wouldn't suit general printing. That market is already well serviced by printers who have the latest equipment and are better at it than us.'

'We should export then,' she said not giving up.

'Its true countries like India with their vast populations will be slow to change but their costs are so much lower we can't compete.'

'Anyway, what you're telling us is just a rumour. It may not be true. We are not going to sell and that is final.'

I wanted to resign and let them get on with it, with their short-sighted attitudes. They could appoint a new MD who could preside over the company's demise, but I couldn't resign. It would send the wrong signals to our customers. They would ask questions.

Why is he leaving?

Why is he working for someone else when he owns a third of the company. There must be something wrong; it will be prudent to move our work to a competitor?

Customer confidence would evaporate effectively killing the company off completely.

I was trapped.

I had met Helen at the Oxford Debating Society continuing the debate long after the speaker had left. Helen had taken the opposing opinion to mine, and we argued late into the night. Up until then we had been strangers but soon became friends then lovers, marrying while still at university, much against both our parents' wishes. We bought a big old farmhouse just outside Belper when I had been appointed Sales Director by my father. It had seen better days, but we were young and idealistic and had dreams of self-sufficiency. We wanted to restore it, so we let the fields out to a local farmer while we worked on the house. He kept our freezer full in exchange for the grazing, which was an amicable arrangement that we never changed. There was always something else to do so self-sufficiency took a back seat as we started a family. We had a wonderful 20 years of family life, domestic bliss, the boys running wild in the fields, helping the farmer with his lambing. Then they left home Colin in the army I knew not where and John at Cambridge probably on his way to America when he graduates.

Helen was lost without the boys to mother anymore, so she went back to her first love, animals. We had had a dog when the boys were young. They loved running in the fields with him or going on the family camping holiday; the dog always sleeping between their sleeping bags. When he died the boys were heartbroken and Helen's instant reaction was we'll get another one. I quickly said, 'No, he was irreplaceable, we wouldn't get another one as good as him'. What I didn't say was that I didn't want a dog in the first place, it was just something Helen turned up with one day and I couldn't say no to the boys. I resented the tie the dog became, never having a holiday abroad because Helen wouldn't put him in kennels because he would get upset. I resented coming down in the morning in bare feet and treading in dog mess; there is nothing like the smell of a dog with the shits.

I could have coped with another man by getting angry; leaving her and starting my life again but it wasn't dogs this time it was horses. Learning to cook was a necessity, otherwise I would have starved, horses came first, second and me a definite last. Even in the evenings we sat in separate rooms Helen with videos of Eventing or The Derby and me with the other TV watching the same old films over and over, then to bed in separate rooms. You could say our marriage was dead, but it wouldn't lie down, or I feared change. Change means making decisions, divorce, not enough money, having to live in a bedsit while the wife keeps the house. It was just easier to carry on, stuck in the rut.

Chapter 2

2nd February 1976.

I had spent the afternoon just outside the city of Lincoln visiting a customer I had promised the earth to for his order, but we delivered the job late. That is a side of the job that others don't see, having to be nice to people you don't like, crawl and say sorry it won't happen again. I ended up taking him and his wife out for dinner. She went on and on about her 'darling' bringing out photograph after photograph which you must smile to and say isn't he wonderful. What is it about women and horses?

Luckily it was an early dinner, as she had to go and put her 'darling' to bed. Now I was on my own time.

We had eaten up by the Cathedral at the Wig and Mitre, more of a restaurant than a pub. Coming out, they turned left to where they had left their car, and I turned right down a cobbled street called Steep Hill towards the high street and my hotel.

I felt the muscles at the front of my legs being stretched on that hill as I tried not to slip on the wet cobbles. The fog was drifting through those ancient streets, and I could imagine knights riding their chargers up this hill with their hooves clattering on the cobbles to the castle next to the cathedral.

At the bottom I stood at a pedestrian crossing completely at a loss about what to do when a glow in the fog to my left attracted me as people hurried past huddled in thick coats against the cold. I don't know why I followed them until the Theatre Royal appeared out of the gloom, but I was glad I did; it looked so warm and inviting. Luckily the box office sold me a half-price ticket as the curtain was going up in five minutes.

I can't remember who the star of the show was but one of the acts was a group of Chinese acrobats. They were amazing as they tumbled across the stage, literally throwing a young woman from one group to another tumbling head over heels as she flew. The finale was a pyramid of all the acrobats held up by just one man with the young woman climbing up to the top over twenty feet off the ground.

It was after the show; while having a drink in the Red Lion the troupe came in chattering away in Chinese and took the table next to mine. The young woman was about 25 or 26 but small in stature being about 5' 2" and very slim. After about ten minutes I drew up enough courage to compliment her on her act. To my astonishment she thanked me in a broad Lancashire accent. Amused at my reaction she introduced herself as Agnes Gilmore and explained that her father was English and her mother Chinese from Hong Kong.

'Will you introduce your husband', I said. Her face changed so quickly, from a laughing happy one full of life, to one so sad it seemed to lose all its colour going almost grey, 'He died', she said, turning back to the group.

'I'm sorry', I blurted out, 'please forgive me'.

Agnes slowly turned around. 'It's not your fault', she said, 'how could you know', Agnes explained that she was not related to anyone in the troupe and had joined them a month ago when their flyer, as she called her, broke her leg. The troupe had appealed to the Chinese Circus School in Manchester who recommended Agnes.

'So, what about you', she asked, 'are you married?' Agnes was a natural listener. Each time I wavered she would ask another question until my life was before her. Things about how I felt, Helen, dogs, work, the customers, the future and the frustration.

The group started to show signs of leaving when Agnes invited me to go with them back to their hotel as they rarely went to bed early. At the hotel the men headed for the hotel bar while Agnes took my hand saying, 'Do you want to come up to my room?'

Did I? I had never been unfaithful to Helen, but we hadn't had sex for over two years we had been like strangers. So yes, I did want to go to her room.

'Why me,' I asked? 'You're a young woman, why not one of your fellow acrobats?'

'That would be impossible. If I had sex with one of them the others would get jealous and I'm not into group sex.'

'But still, why me?'

'Since my husband died, I've been suffering from depression and sex helps me to forget, even if it is just for a short time. The nights make me feel bad when the door closes and I'm all alone. As for it being you. You are here, now. You're pleasant and there is no one else. Don't take that as an insult but you are nearly old enough to be my father.'

As we entered the room Agnes said, 'I had a shower at the theatre, you need to have one. Turn the light out before you leave the bathroom and let your eyes adjust to the dark.

The sight I saw when I came back in will always stay in my mind. There were so many candles the room glowed, and a soft oriental music was playing but what had my attention was Agnes. She was not beautiful, not even pretty she was simply erotic; sex radiated from her.

'Bugger', I said, looking at the clock, it was past 10. I was supposed to be on my way to Cardiff for a meeting. Telephoning the office, I told them I had eaten something last night that had me up all night with hardly a wink of sleep and they were to cancel my appointments for the rest of the week.

'You were telling me yesterday about what you do, it sounds exciting,' she said.

'I wouldn't say it was exciting; I find it interesting trying to think like a criminal saying to oneself 'How would I break the system and steal the money;' then finding a way to prevent it?'

'Has there ever been something you couldn't stop?'

'Yes and No,' I said.

'Now you're intriguing me, you can't stop there.'

'I found a scam that was so big the criminals would take millions. I told the group who were at risk, but they are taking no action to prevent it.'

'Why is that?'

'There is no quick fix. It would cost them several million and take a good ten years to roll out. Anyway, they are convinced it won't happen as it would need an army of criminals all over the country to do the same thing at the same time. How could that happen?'

'What did you mean last night, when you said that I made love like an Englishman', I said, 'I am English'.

'I didn't say you made love like an Englishman I said you had sex like one. You're confusing the two; anyone can have sex but only people in love make love. Humans are the only species that can enjoy sexual pleasure just for its sheer enjoyment; with all other species it's about reproduction, the next generation.

Western men don't think about the girl under them and just bang away until they are satisfied,' she explained. 'I'm told that many English women never experience an orgasm.'

I was dumbstruck, mostly because I was not expecting such a frank outburst, and it must have shown on my face.

'It's not your fault', she said quickly, 'it's your Victorian culture'.

'You'll have to Explain', I said.

'An Eastern mother teaches her daughter how to please a man by joining in and getting as much pleasure as he does. She teaches that sex is something to be enjoyed not just endured. When a boy reaches 18 yrs an uncle or close male relative will take him to the local whorehouse where his sexual education will be given on how to please a woman. A good sexual relationship in marriage will make it a stable one. That's why there are so many Chinese in the world, and why China had to impose a one child family policy?' she said.

'Most Western mothers don't even talk about sex to their daughters if they tell them anything at all it's that men need sex, it is their driving force. It is what they work all their life for even before they put a roof over their heads and food in their bellies.

It's what they think about when they wake up and when they go to sleep. You just must endure it so you can have children', she said. 'So, a lot of Western girls just lie on their backs and let the man get on with it.

Men are voyeurs, they get turned on by looking at a woman's body, that's why there are so many girly magazines in the shops. Appeal to their eyes and women will have a great relationship with their man, he has no self-control he can't turn off his desire A woman must start to turn on a man with the WOW factor.'

'That's very cynical.'

'No, it's the truth and it's about time people faced it. I bet you learned about sex behind the bike sheds at school.'

'Well, I...........'

'That's what I thought. The English are not taught about relationships between a man and a woman.

An English couple get married then fumble around in the dark; neither of them knowing what to do just following their instincts. An Englishman is embarrassed talking about sex unless they're bragging to their mates. A typical English parent just closes their eyes expecting the schools to teach their kids. That's the way to unwanted child pregnancies and ruined lives.

Now you're on sick leave what are you doing for the rest of the week', she asked.

'I think you might have an idea about that', I said.

'We're here for the next three days, then we go on to Norwich; stay with me', she said.

'Great', I said.

I booked out of the Marriot and moved in with her. Each evening, I watched the performance from the wings and each night Agnes taught me things about sex I had never imagined existed.

The last night was the best and yet it was sad. We both knew it would be the last day, never to be repeated. Agnes did not want a lasting relationship with a married man 20 years older than her.

'You're a very unusual woman Agnes. I have never known anyone to be so frank about what they feel. All the women I have known kept their thoughts to themselves. They certainly didn't talk about sex or tell me what they would like me to do.'

'That's sad', said Agnes, 'all those wasted nights, all that wasted pleasure.

Are you going to the ACPO at GMEX next month? I hope you don't mind but I spoke to my father last night and told him about you and your work; he would like to meet you. The Professor, as we all call him, is presenting a paper and hopes you can attend then talk to him afterwards. You can do some networking; you might even pick up some new customers. My sister, Amanda will be there as she's Dad's assistant, I'll tell her to look out for you'.

'The Professor,' I asked?

'Dad is an Honorary Professor of Criminology at Manchester University; his speciality is 'Organised Crime and Gang Culture'. Amanda is The Professor's Girl Friday. She was going to get married two years ago but her fiancé had an accident a week before the wedding and died', she said, 'she never got over it'.

I went into the office the next day only to be told to go home again as I looked like death warmed up. I did not tell them the real reason I looked so drained.

Chapter 3

GMEX[1] was one of the great railway stations of the steam age, until it became redundant. They could have just pulled it down but instead it was refurbished into a conference centre and is fantastic for concerts as the acoustics are wonderful.

The ACPO[2] conference took place on Wednesday and Thursday and took up the whole of GMEX which is quite something. They had the main lecture area and two workshops going for the delegates from all the regional police forces. There were also quite a few delegates from other countries and Interpol, making it an international gathering.

Around the sides of the hall were trade stands selling everything a policeman could want from fast cars to body armour and guns. Heckler and Koch had a shooting range with electronic targets. I never realised how difficult it is for an officer to decide in a split second whether to shoot or not. When I had a go, I'm afraid I shot a civilian and the bank robber shot me.

According to the programme Professor Gilmore would be presenting his paper 'The War on Drugs, Prostitution and Organised Crime' the next day in the main hall so I spent the day networking and picked up some possible leads.

---

[1] Greater Manchester Exhibition Centre
[2] Association of Chief Police Officers

The following day was sunny and dry but a bit cold after a sharp frost. The steps leading up to the main entrance gleamed in the sunshine as if they had just been washed. Delegates were streaming from all directions, and security was even tighter than the previous day as there had been an IRA bomb threat.

I met an ACC[3] from yesterday and he told me about his problems while I waited for the lecture to begin. I find it very useful when people do that, then I can come up with a system to solve it for them. Quite often I can sell a lot of security forms that way but only if it solves the problem. Sometimes I advise them to change the internal system and give them advice. I don't necessarily make a sale, but it enhances my reputation of being honest and next time they have a problem they give me a call first, when I do make that sale.

A bell rang to announce the start of the morning session, and we all sat down in the lecture area. There was a table to the left of the stage where the Chairman sat with his committee. It was angled so if they looked left they could see the large screen high up behind the stage and a lectern and microphone on the other side for the speaker. Looking right they could see the audience.

---

[3] Assistant Chief Constable

The Chairman walked across to the lectern where he tapped the mike twice and a dull boom echoed through the hall.

'Ladies and Gentlemen', he said, 'This morning's speaker is well known to all of us by his controversial reputation. He is here today to put those ideas to you direct and answer your questions in person. I invite the Honorary Professor of Criminology of Manchester University to address us on 'The War on Drugs, Prostitution and Organised Crime', Professor Gilmore'.

The professor was quite a short man but strutted like a fighting cock up to the Chairman and shook hands. He was about 5' 6" tall with a mop of white hair and a goatee. The chairman's 6-foot plus towered over him but appeared insignificant as the Professor's huge personality dominated everything. His brown tweed jacket had seen better days as it had been mended with leather patches at elbows and cuffs. He looked like a caricature of the academic he was, and his head should have been surrounded by a cloud of pipe smoke. During the Leckture he actually pulled out a pipe from his pocket and used it as a pointer to the screen to emphasise a point.

The Chairman went to his seat at the table as the Professor went to the lectern and after a short pause commenced his paper.

I can't remember all the Professor's paper or describe the many slides and statistics the Professor presented to support his case, but this is much as I can recall. I believe the following conveys the essence of the Professor's presentation.

The War on Drugs, Prostitution and Organised Crime

In my many years as a policeman I fought the twin cancers that are drugs and prostitution, in the military, in the police in Hong Kong and here in this country. I know from first-hand the horror of drugs when a good friend was ruined by the poppy, and I have seen young women and girls sold or kidnapped into a life of prostitution. I could not kill these cancers for every time I removed a piece from society another took its place.

They are still growing in strength; drugs are ruining this and the next generation; and the one after that can be born already addicted from their mother's womb. The sex industry is blighting our cities with their shops and massage parlours while prostitutes walk the streets and kerb crawlers approach our innocent women by mistake.

We will never eradicate these cancers for mankind is weak but why are they growing? It's because they are in the hands of the organised criminal. We must take control away from the criminal, not to defeat the cancers but to control them and we will never do this by locking up its victims.

Prostitution is often known as the oldest profession in the world. It could be argued that this is because men are weak and driven by base instincts and there are some women who will use their charms to take advantage of it to make money.

It is something the criminal gets involved in because it is illegal, and they can make large profits. Many prostitutes' parade on street corners looking for punters lowering the value of many a property or area.

The criminal does not care about the welfare of the girls or that they are one of the biggest sources for sexually communicated diseases. In many cases the girls are sold by starving families so the rest can live a little longer or even abducted into a life of slavery. Perhaps they are deliberately made addicts by pimps, so they are forced to turn to prostitution to feed their habit.

It could be said that it is a stain on society, but I would also argue that prostitution provides a valuable service to society as it can act as a safety valve for man's sexual needs. Preventing them taking their frustration out on their wife or partner or even going out and raping some innocent. They also provide a useful source of information for the police as they are told or overhear many a secret.

Let us all agree drugs are the scourge of society. They ruin peoples' lives, destroy families and cost society billions in prevention and treatment. Society's answer is to ban drugs by making them illegal and locking up those involved. However, one should learn from history that this does not work.

A criminal is a businessman and is quite happy to stand outside schools giving free samples until the children become hooked then the price goes up. The children start by stealing from their parents, emptying the bank accounts and credit cards, progressing onto burglary, car theft and a life of crime. At the other end of the supply chain are the Afghan Warlords and Colombian drug cartels enforcing their rule with Kalashnikovs, murdering thousands. Countries like the UK and USA spend billions trying to stop the trade without success for as one group is put behind bars another takes its place. The profit is too large for it to stop.

Let us try to put the whole thing into perspective by listing some of the costs in the supply chain.

Starving Afghan farmers grow the opium poppy and Colombian's cocaine as it's the best way of feeding their families or the cartels or warlords give them no choice. Then the army comes along destroying the crop, the farmer and their family starve leaving the cartels intact or if destroyed replaced by another.

The raw material is converted and shipped into the user countries by every ingenious means possible. The DEA, Customs Officers or anti-drug agents track the shipments or stand on the borders like the 7th cavalry protecting Custer. However, just like the 7th they get some of the Indians, but many get through until they are overwhelmed.

Now the local gangs get involved cutting the 'pure' with powdered sugar, talcum powder or chalk, if the users are lucky or rat poison or powdered glass if they are not, until it is diluted to a usable level for a fix.

We must not forget the human cost of those being burgled with higher house insurance or mugged for a few pounds only to find themselves in hospital. The NHS spends millions more treating the addicts' victims and the users made brain dead by overdosing on badly refined or cut drugs.

There are many costs, many of which cannot be quantified, but we do know that it costs the UK economy in one way or another billions, however the worst is the human misery.

Drug misuse has no redeeming qualities it is a cancer in society, spreading around the world. It does not respect class, creed or wealth. It destroys families, it destroys lives, it touches everyone in the world in higher taxes to combat the cancer and pay the NHS to treat the victims or higher insurance premiums.

I would like to illustrate the extent of the problem like this', he said, turning to the screen.

> *A map of the World appeared*

'Let's enlarge the map and go in closer to Manchester. Now to a night club where an 18-year-old is dancing, enjoying her hen party.

> *A street in Manchester now appeared*

Let's call her Jane Smith. What she doesn't know is this is not her last day of being single; it is the last day of her life. She is encouraged to snort cocaine for the first time in her life as a last rebellious act before a lifetime of commitment. But it has been badly cut and she overdoses. This black cross on the map represents her death.

> *The map enlarged to Manchester with black crosses appearing all over the city.*

'These are the other lives wasted in a single year in Manchester as a direct result of illegal drug misuse. It is like a plague across the city; each one represents a family devastated; a family in mourning for the loss of a loved one. Let us zoom in again to just outside a school gate this time in Cardiff.

> *Another street showing an outline of a school*

A 14-year-old has been selling drugs to his classmates. The local pusher confronts the 14-year-old who pulls out a knife and stabs the pusher to death. These are all victims, the pusher who is dead, the 14-year-old who will probably spend much of his life institutionalised and the children, many of whom will become lifelong addicts.

> *The map zoomed out again to show the whole of Cardiff as crosses for this sort of death were added*

Now we add the deaths from gang wars; the drug barons enforcing their will; the fights with the police resisting arrest and the police knifed or shot trying to stop this dreadful trade; all of these are victims of the cancer. But it is not just Manchester or Cardiff', continued the Professor, 'let us see the UK and all the major cities.

> *The Map of UK now showed the cities showing as dark shapes*

We'll now add those crimes that are the next level. The ones committed to feed the cancer. The burglaries and car thefts but just the crimes reported to the police not the thousands of thefts from the family that are never reported. It is estimated that an addict needs between £15,000 and £20,000 a year to feed their habit and there are about 300,000 heroin addicts in the UK. If they only get one third of the value for the goods they obtain by theft, burglary, fraud or shoplifting it will total at about £2 – 2.5 billion or half of the recorded crime in the UK.

> *The cities were now completely black with grey spreading into the countryside*

However, this is not a solely UK problem.

> *The map zoomed out again to the World view; black spreading across the map from East to West from North to South; from Afghanistan and Columbia to the USA and Europe*

This is a modern-day cancer that is killing our children. It is orchestrated, developed and promoted by organised criminal gangs worldwide. It spreads from the Poppy fields of Afghanistan and the Cocaine fields of Columbia to your door.

Human nature means that 'mankind' is insecure and weak; 'mankind' will always need something to lean on or make him feel better. This could be drugs, sex, alcohol, nicotine, gambling or religion. Criminals form themselves into gangs, as a gang can dominate an individual or area taking advantage of our human needs or fears. Anything that is illegal but wanted by the people is an opportunity for the criminal.

We will not defeat drug abuse until we can change human nature. As it is impossible to change human nature it is impossible to defeat drug abuse.

The 'War on Drugs and Prostitution' is lost before it has started'.

This would seem the end of the lecture, but we need to address these problems, not ignore them, and if we cannot eradicate them, we must at least reduce their effect on society and control them.

I propose that we take away the food that is feeding this cancer (profit) and clean up our streets by legalising both prostitution and hard drugs. To legalise alone would send the wrong message; the key is 'Control and Educate'.

We can use a criminal's own greed to redirect them into activities that have a less devastating effect on society. Criminals are first and foremost businessmen and are looking for the greatest profit for the least effort. They may enforce their contract terms a little more directly than say the bank, but if things become difficult their human nature is to look for something that is easier for the same profit. There will always be the psychopaths and the criminally insane and there is nothing to do with them but keep them away from society.

We must learn from American history. In the 30's they made alcohol illegal, and the likes of Capone took over as they could make large profits. As soon as it was legalised the criminals lost interest as the profits vanished, and the authorities regained control.

That is what we must do, 'Decriminalise, Control and Educate'.

To control prostitution each town or city council needs to provide enclosed premises that are away from habitation. Sex shops and massage parlours to be moved inside the complex away from our city streets and into this enclosed secure environment. The prostitutes to be registered, licensed, medically examined weekly and working there by their own free will. The enterprise formed into a co-operative financed by the prostitutes giving a portion of their takings for maternity leave and health care and paying income tax, like every other citizen.

To control the drug problem the pharmaceutical companies to contract with the

Afghan and Columbian farmers to grow opium or cocaine for legal use. Import the raw materials and refine under pharmaceutical control. Distribute at their true price through dedicated shops. Move the convicted addicts from prison to treatment centres and rehabilitate the users back into society rather than be a blight on it. This will also reduce the pressure on the Prison Service, who wouldn't need to build new prisons.

A high-profile advertising campaign to be mounted and an educational programme to be maintained in all schools encouraging peer pressure against drug misuse.

To summarise; widespread uncontrolled prostitution and drug misuse is ruining our society. Many would argue that decriminalising them would send the wrong message. This would be the case if that were all that we did. We would be educating this and the next generation against misuse and the consequences if they do.

The NHS would cost less, as would the Police and the Prison Service, the Chancellor of the Exchequer would receive more tax revenue; the national crime rate would drop like a stone as the police concentrated their resources on other crimes and society would improve. While our innocent women would be free to walk the streets knowing they are not going to be molested by curb crawlers.

Spend the billions saved from prevention, on education about the misuse of drugs and rehabilitating users as having an illness and not locking them up. You will never stop everyone using but stopping most, especially children becoming the next generation of users is the aim.

Spend the rest of the money saved on the causes of the need for a prop to survive life's hardships like good housing, jobs, education and over-population.

The Professor then thanked the audience for their forbearance for listening to his controversial paper.

At this point the Chairman went to the centre of the stage thanking Professor Gilmore for his thought-provoking paper asking for any questions from the floor.

'The Chair recognises the Assistant Chief Constable of Devon', said the chairman.

"Professor", she said, 'This is a political solution you are proposing. So should you not address it to parliament?'

'Yes, it is', replied the Professor, 'but politics involves all of us not the just politicians. They will not act unless they are convinced by the police, NHS and all other parties involved that it could work. My proposal is controversial, but it can work. The alternative is to carry on as we are with spiralling costs and bigger prisons to lock away our mistakes'.

As the first questioner sat down the chairman said, 'The Chair recognises the Chief Constable of Greater Manchester'.

'I'm afraid your proposal for the drugs problem is a non-starter Professor', he said. 'You would never get all the countries to agree, there are too many people involved either living in fear or bribed to look the other way'.

'You are correct, that is why the UK should lead the way. If we can eliminate the market here the criminals will move their efforts to other countries. The domino effect would then take over as each country followed our lead until the world-wide problem was controlled. Involving other countries as we do now and attacking the producers and the supply chain does not work. The War on Drugs is lost. We must find an alternative; take away the market and the whole trade would dry up. It would not happen overnight but take many years, but we must succeed for the sake of our children.'

The questions kept coming for a further 20 minutes until the Chairman intervened thanking the Professor once more and declared the morning session over.

Lunch was an informal affair at the back of the hall. People were lining up at two long tables set up on either side with identical offerings. First one collected a plate and cutlery from a pile at the end then progressed down the tables with serving staff offering a variety of cold dishes from salmon to quiche followed by salad with rice or couscous. One then had to find a seat amongst the randomly placed tables. There was a table of two foreign police officers and a British Chief Constable with a spare chair so asked if I could join them. After a nod from them I sat down. One then had to repeat the process all over again for the sweet course and coffee.

As we sat the three police officers discussed the Professor's proposal from different angles. All seemed to agree that it had merit but felt that the politicians would not agree as they seemed only to be interested in retaining their jobs. The consensus was that they could not see such a radical action getting the go ahead as it would upset too many voters, even if the police backed it.

It was while I was drinking coffee that I looked up to see a group standing in a circle holding their plates and trying to eat while talking to a central figure. They were all looking down and by their animation could only be talking to the Professor. Beside the Professor was another figure but all I could see was a golden ponytail flicking from side to side as the person turned to look at whoever was speaking. It shone like a golden hand waving to me for although the group were in shadow a shaft of sunlight came down through the glass roof, lighting her hair. As I watched, the group parted, and I saw a tall lithe woman in her prime standing in that pool of sunlight. She was about 5' 9" and wearing heels that made her the same height as those around her. She was wearing a simple blouse and skirt that ended just above the knee, but she filled it superbly, not voluptuous and not thin either, just superbly. She turned, looked directly at me and smiled such a smile that the hall seemed to glow. Walking towards me her legs seemed to go on forever as they swung gracefully to her hip movement, not that her hips were over large, but her narrow waist emphasised her womanly shape. I stood as she approached holding out her hand. 'I'm Amanda', she said, 'you must be Joe. Agnes described you perfectly.'

Chapter 4

Amanda put her arm through mine and her touch was like static electricity it made my whole being tingle. Guiding me towards the group the uniformed figures parted like waves before her.

'Professor,' she said, 'can I introduce Joe'.

'Joe, very pleased to meet you at last, Agnes has told us all about you', he said.

Not 'all' I hoped.

'What did you think of my proposal?' he asked.

'You put a very strong case', I said, 'I think it would work but would the politicians agree'?

'That's the problem', he agreed, 'none of them has the balls. It would take a million people writing to their MP[4] before anything happened'.

At that point the bell rang for the afternoon session, so we headed back to our seats. Amanda touched my arm saying, 'Why don't you join us?'

With great pleasure, I did.

I can't remember much about the Chairman's paper on 'Policing in the late 20th Century', as my mind kept coming back to the fabulous creature beside me.

---

[4] Member of Parliament

The chairman's closing remarks went over my head and I found us heading for the exit.

The Professor turned to me saying, 'Agnes has told me about your work in security documents, and I would like to pick your brain. I like to learn as much as I can from experts about what criminals get up to. It helps me understand their motivations and how they may react in different circumstances.'

'Of course,' I said.

'There are too many ears around to discuss anything here. What are you doing this weekend?'

'Not much', I said.

'We are going up to Windermere to my boat, why don't you join us' he asked?

My mind was a whirl, Helen, not the right clothes, the whole weekend crammed in a small cruiser with Amanda and her father. I just managed to get out, 'Yes, I would love to'.

Rather than go home for a change of clothes I went straight to the Lakes staying in Kendall at a B & B. The clothing problem was solved at an outdoors shop by some walking trousers, tee shirts, rubber soled shoes and a thick jumper to keep out the cold. Amanda had said to turn up about 10 so following her directions I arrived at the mooring to find row upon row of boats wrapped up for the winter like small animals huddling together for warmth. One boat had activity as I saw the Professor washing the deck with a mop. I think he was trying to get the wet leaves off the deck that had fallen from the surrounding trees as he kept dipping the mop into the water then swinging it up pushing all before him over the edge.

'Hi', I called, 'Do you want a hand with that'.

Turning, the Professor replied, 'Thank you but I've just finished. If you don't get the leaves off it stains the paintwork, then it's twice as hard to keep it white'.

'Come aboard, were ready to get going'. He called into the wheelhouse, 'Amanda, Joe's here. Show him his cabin then give me a hand with the mooring ropes'.

'I'll do it', I called as I dropped my bag on the deck.

'Let go the bow rope first and give me a push off', he called. 'I'll swing out on the stern rope so I can get past the boat in front'.

Running forward I untied the mooring rope and threw it aboard then leaned against the boat. The bow slowly moved away so I inched towards the stern pushing as I went. The Professor started the engines which swung the bows out even more as I held the boat on the stern mooring rope. Seeing the bow was clear I undid the stern rope and climbed aboard.

'You've done that before', said Amanda.

'A holiday on the Norfolk Broads,' I replied as I turned to find her standing on the deck watching me. The thick padded coat hid her figure, but nothing could disguise those long slender legs encased in tight jeans.

We went forward to the wheelhouse to find the Professor standing on a box at the steering wheel so he could see out the windscreen. He saw me looking at the box and laughed.

'Many people think Amanda was adopted but her mother was 6ft and she has her physical shape but my brains. The height difference never mattered to us, it's what's inside that counts', he said. 'Ju, Agnes's mother, can look me in the eye. Ju means Chrysanthemum flower and like the flower she is perfect in every way, Agnes takes after her. Ju gets motion sickness easily, even on these calm waters and would rather stay at home. So, Amanda and I normally have the boat to ourselves'.

I needn't have worried about being cramped; the Professor's boat was positively spacious. I found out later it was a 50ft Silver Classic Motor Sailer, a wooden sailing boat, built in 1937. There were three cabins, one for each of us. Originally it would have slept eight, but the centre cabins had been converted to a large salon with a table in the middle surrounded by chairs like a board room, which seemed strange. It was 50ft long 11 ft. 5 in wide (beam) with a draft of 3ft 6 in. Two masts for sailing, each Bermuda rigged, or did that make it a Ketch, or you could use the twin engine/twin screws for cruising. The hull was white as was the deck and the varnish in the enclosed wheelhouse glowed golden in the sunshine and the brass-work gleamed. It must have cost a fortune; I could only think that Professors must be very well paid. There was even a bath which the Professor could probably sit in with legs outstretched. Amanda and I would have to stand up and use the shower. The advantage for both of us was that the standing headroom throughout was over 6ft so we were not cracking our skulls while below.

Leaving the other boats behind in the deserted mooring, we motored across the mere. The water was like glass with not a ripple. A cold damp mist was in the air so you could not tell where water met mist or mist met sky. In a very short time, we seemed to be the only boat on the water as the mist became thicker to become a fog, and the Professor said we had better drop anchor until it cleared. With the engine stopped we just sat there in silence with the fog forming a shroud about the boat. There was no sound, no birds no creaking of the boat, no slapping of halyards, nothing except the odd sound of a car going along the lakeside road to Bowness-on-Windermere. We waited with some trepidation for some idiot to appear out of the fog and ram us. The Professor said that we were away from the main routes, but you never know if someone is lost but keeps going rather than anchor.

It could have been very boring just sitting there but time just slipped by as the Professor told us about his time in the army as a Military Police Captain in Singapore. Then with the fall of Singapore how the British and Australian soldiers marched into captivity. The Japanese never understood that and treated them worse than animals as they had nothing but contempt for anyone who surrendered. A Japanese soldier would die rather than surrender, he gave his life to his Emperor when he became a soldier, and his family put up a shrine to their dead hero son never expecting to see him again.

Amanda made coffee and we stood on the deck as the steam rose in the air from our mugs to join the fog that surrounded us. Not a sound, just utter stillness; we could have been six feet from shore or sixty.

'Will you tell us what happened after the war,' I asked?'

'All the time I was a prisoner the one thing that kept me sane was that I knew my wife and unborn child were safe, probably in Australia, for that was where the ship I put her on, the Orient Star, was heading. We were finally released in October 1945 a month after Japan surrendered and flown direct to Australia for treatment. I lay in that bed for two weeks until they would let me up. Two weeks of hell, not of the wounds but of guilt. The guilt of surviving when so many others had died. The irony was that a month before half the camp had been emptied and shipped to Japan in unmarked transports, what were later called death ships; only this one was sunk by one of our own submarines and the prisoners drowned. Why was I spared? Why did I live? I still don't know to this day. I think it was just luck. Luck that I didn't get beriberi or dysentery. Luck that one of the guards didn't like my face one day and stick a bayonet in me.

It took three months for our bodies to adjust to eating normal food. First it was intravenous drips and baby food or thin soup, anything stronger and we threw it up. Gradually we put on weight and got our strength back, the uniforms they gave us just flapped around us; the quartermaster didn't have anything small enough to fit our emaciated bodies.

As soon as I was able, I contacted ANTC[5] to find out which harbour the Orient Star docked at and where the passengers went. They searched their records but found nothing. They contacted New Guinea and all other possible ports with the same result. However, they said they would keep searching and not to give up hope, as many records had been lost or just misfiled. I couldn't understand it. The ship got away I saw it sail. Two weeks later there was a call from ANTC asking me to visit their office.

The orderly got me a driver and that ride nearly killed me as I am sure the driver was mad or had a death wish. I was shown into a captain's office and

---

[5] Australian Naval Transport Command

after saluting like a 90-year-old I collapsed into a chair utterly drained. After the formalities were completed and a mug of navy tea with a good slug of rum the officer went on to explain that the Orient Star never made it. However, he had a report from another ship that had left Singapore at the same time, that they saw the ship torpedoed two days out. They only picked up one boat of survivors but couldn't stay to pick up any more for fear of being sunk themselves. The captain reported that one of the women in the boat was pregnant but had died giving birth to a baby girl. A French Nun called Sister Agnès had cared for the baby girl but nothing more was known. It may have been my wife or just a coincidence.

It took me another two years to find out that Sister Agnès had returned to a closed order in France. The letters to the order went unanswered so I went to the convent in the Dordogne. At first the Mother Superior refused to see me, but I persuaded the Priest, who took their confessions, to plead my case. It took him nearly six months to persuade the Mother Superior that it would be God's wish that the child be united with its only living parent. She therefore agreed that Sister Agnès could have special dispensation to talk to me about the child she helped to bring into the world but nothing else.

Sister Agnès had cared for the baby and called her Amanda but when she had to return to her order she placed Amanda in an orphanage in Australia.

She had left with the child her mother's necklace containing pictures of her mother and father. She said that she could not be sure, but she thought the picture could have been me.

Amanda was nearly six by the time I found her, not in the orphanage but with foster parents. I turned up with a photograph of myself and my wife when we were younger that matched the necklace that Amanda still had. The foster parents were happy for Amanda finally being with her father but equally dismayed, for they had planned to adopt her.

I was demobbed from the army and went to Hong Kong and joined the Colonial Police Service where I eventually became Assistant Chief Constable. I met Ju and we married and had a little girl who we named after Sister Agnès.

We didn't want to stay in Hong Kong when it passed back to Chinese control, so I managed to get a transfer to Manchester Police and later, when I retired, I was offered an Honorary Professorship at Manchester University.'

The fog had finally cleared, and we motored up to the north of Windermere where we anchored for lunch. Amanda proved she was no slouch in the galley if not inventive, bacon butties with lots of strong tea and fruit cake.

The afternoon was just as pleasurable as we cruised around the mere while the Professor told me about the chap who built a mock castle on the lakeside with his wife's money but when it was finished, she didn't like it and refused to stay in it.

It was getting dark about 4 o'clock so we went back to the mooring and relaxed in the boat's lounge where the Professor brought out a bottle of Scotch.

'To keep out the cold', he said.

He continued telling us stories of his early life in Hong Kong as a policeman up against the Tongs but never once mentioned the long years in prison-of-war camps again.

We talked about my job with documents, and he was very interested in what we did to make them secure. I explained that there are two types of features. Overt, these are ones you can see like the design with a background of wavy lines like a banknote and there are Covert features that you can't see.

All these things are difficult to reproduce, not impossible for if one person can make it so can someone else with the expertise and enough money. It's about balance you need to spend enough money protecting what you need to. This could be access to your system or building with a pass or money in the form of cash, cheques or bearer bonds. But you don't want to spend more protecting what you are trying to keep safe than what it's worth.

It's as you said in your lecture Professor we cannot stop the criminal. We just make the effort of breaking into the system not worth it, so they go and attack someone else's. It sounds cynical but its reality.'

'It's that expertise Agnes knew I would be interested in', said the Professor. 'She said you visit customers and tell them how you would break their systems then sell them something to protect them; that's clever. She also said you had come across a scam you couldn't prevent.'

'That's true but it won't happen for as well as the usual technical difficulties there are two major problems', I said.

'I would still like to hear about it as Agnes told me it would be a national event that would involve organised crime and that's my specialty.'

'Before I do I need to put the whole thing into context, so bear with me.

Some criminals steal original documents then alter the information; that's forgery. Others counterfeit documents, that means they manufacture a complete document from scratch.

The main source for original documents is to steal them while they're in transit such as the Post Office. Others are stolen from a handbag or wallet. The Post Office is supposed to be secure, but it leaks like a sieve. There was an incident recently where a worker in the sorting office was approached to steal credit cards. They're easy to spot, the banks tend to use a certain type of envelope or design on the outside, one day they will get smart and put them in the same envelope they use for ordinary post.

He was told if he side-tracked a card, he would get £500; if it was a gold card, he would get £1000. His initial reaction was that he wouldn't do it, then it was pointed out that his son had a very lonely walk to school, and wouldn't it be tragic if he had a serious accident; what was the father to do. It's happening now and will continue. If you add up all the thefts, it's very substantial but it's not organised on a national scale. The same goes for counterfeiting, one of the main areas now are vehicle documents. The documents don't have to be good as you are only trying to fool a member of the public. If the MOT certificate is not quite right the public is not going to notice, and you can sell a dodgy car.

You can't steal enough documents to make it worthwhile and if you did the producers would soon spot that they had gone missing and change the design so the ones you had stolen would become so much wastepaper. The answer is to print your own copies or counterfeit. To do a sustained attack your documents need to be good quality because they are being seen by people who are trained on what to look for; this is why attempts in the past have failed. If you can't make the quality required, they will be spotted in a couple of days. If you can only pass a few hundred before being apprehended; it's not worthwhile.

It's like selling, you can either sell a Rolls Royce for a £million or you can sell 10 million cans of beans for 10p per can. You end up with a £million whichever way you do it. A criminal can't make a document with high quality to steal a large amount of money such as bearer bonds, but he can make a lower quality one in large numbers, but it would soon be spotted. The secret is to find the weak link. The point in the targets amour where they wouldn't spot the lower quality, just accept them as genuine.'

'So, what is it,' the Professor demanded getting irritable.

'It's Gift Vouchers. Millions are printed each year and every big shop in the country uses them to increase sales, especially at Christmas. The shops love them as about 25% are never redeemed so the shops are just printing money for themselves. Counter staff have some training on spotting counterfeit cash and gift vouchers but the people with the greatest knowledge are in the back office. As soon as the cash and vouchers leave the tills the back office are looking for counterfeits using such things as UV[6] lights. One day the shops will cotton on that it would be a good investment to have the UV lamps at the tills and catch the duds before they

---

[6] Ultraviolet

sell the goods. You see ordinary paper has additives to make it whiter like washing powder makes your shirt whiter, that's why your shirt glows in the UV lights when you go into a dance hall. Hold up any security document to a UV lamp and you will see the paper doesn't glow as they haven't put in the additives, but you do see designs the human eye cannot see. It's a very good feature and hard to reproduce. As soon as a counterfeit is spotted, they tell the other shops. Within a day or so all the salespeople are re-trained on what to look for and the criminals are caught.

If you could make a perfect counterfeit voucher the shops wouldn't know about it for months. As it is nearly impossible to make a perfect voucher the shops have got complacent and don't have adequate accounting procedures. With some shop chains when you buy a voucher in one store, they put the money into a special account; when you redeem the voucher at another store they take the money out of the account. If you attacked that store group, the first they would know about it was when there wasn't enough money in the account to pay the second store. Some store groups don't even bother to do that, and the money just gets absorbed in the general accounts; these would never know they had been hit.

'Tell me about the threat'.

'There is a way you wouldn't need the quality just a reasonable facsimile and rely on a Smash and

Grab as a poorer quality would be spotted after a few hours. But a Smash and Grab of such scale that it would dwarf anything that has been done before.'

'You're only talking £50 may be £100 at a time. It's just not worth it', said the Professor sounding disappointed.

'The answer is to print or counterfeit on mass and hit every store in the country at the same time.

If you could print millions of vouchers for all the stores, then stockpile them in secret. You could distribute them to the front-line people at Christmas, the ones who would present them at the shops.'

'Why Christmas', he asked?

'The Boxing Day Sales', I replied. 'I assume the front-line people would be mainly drug addicts, who would first sell as many as they could in pubs and clubs on Christmas Eve say at two thirds their face value explaining they were from a relation but what they really need is a fix. The rest they pass in the shops when they open on the first day of the Sales. They need to be passed within the first two hours of the shops opening when there are big crowds and many legitimate ones being exchanged. After that the vouchers would be in the back office and spotted. The longer they keep passing counterfeits the higher the risk of being caught.

That is the shops 'weak link'. There will be many poorly trained Saturday staff serving and the full-time staff will be overwhelmed. Some of the addicts will be caught and some of the punters they sold them to in the pubs but at least 90% won't. If caught all they say, is they bought them from some man in a pub on Christmas Eve; the most they would get is a slap on the wrist.

It would all be over long before they even knew they had been taken in the biggest smash and grab in history. They would lose millions.'

'You say millions; how much do you estimate,' he asked?

'In round figures £75 million; that's not all profit for the criminal. However, that's better than normal when they would only get a third of the value for stolen goods, but as these goods would all have legitimate receipts, guarantees, warranties, etc. their resale value would be much higher than normal stolen property; in many cases they could even take the goods back for a full refund. They should clear in total about 70-75% of that, say, £50 - £60 million,' I replied.

'What defence do the shops have,' asked the Professor?

'None in the short term', I said. 'Long term, the shops need to upgrade their tills to EPOS[7] systems. Then print every voucher with a barcode and link all the EPOS machines to a central computer; where

---

[7] Electronic Point of Sale

every voucher would be logged; recording when and where it was sold and redeemed. That way any fraudulent or duplicate number would be instantly picked up at the till. If the shops decided to protect themselves, it would take them about 10 - 15 years to install and cost millions to do so. But I can't see it happening unless they had serious motivation'.

'So why wouldn't it happen,' asked the Professor?

'Two reasons. The first is the sheer volume involved. You would need a big printing press to print the quantities. This would be quickly spotted, and you couldn't just print £50 vouchers. If the tills suddenly were getting large volumes of £50 vouchers they would smell a rat. You would need a mix of high and low. £100s, £50s, even some £20s so you might end up printing 3 or 4 million vouchers. You would then have to print gift cards and stick them in. That is how grandma sends her gift voucher to little Johnny. So that's another 2 million bits of paper as you must present the document in the way the recipient expects it. If you don't, it doesn't feel right, and they start looking harder.'

'And the second reason,' asked the Professor.

'Cooperation; the only people who could hit every store in the country at the same time are the criminal gangs and as you said it yourself the UK gangs are at each other's throats. All the gangs would have to do the same thing at the same time over the whole country. In total secrecy with no one informing to the police. It wouldn't happen.'

That evening, I took the Professor and Amanda out for a meal at the New Hall Inn at the Hole in t' Wall. One of the Professor's favourites he said if you like steak pie and real ale.

Walking back from the restaurant to the car the professor said he had a confidential meeting the next day on the boat; Amanda and I would need to go out for the day. My business associates like to meet here as its neutral territory and by anchoring out in the middle of the mere there would be no eavesdroppers, but he didn't elaborate further.

Amanda suggested that we went the next day up into the hills for a picnic.

'I don't have the right clothing or any boots', I said.

'That's soon sorted out,' said Amanda, 'there's a slop chest on the boat with all sorts of clothing. There might even be some boots that will fit.'

The next morning the weather was good with no fog. Amanda made up some sandwiches and flasks of coffee while I raided the slop chest; borrowing a padded coat, gloves, woolly hat and walking boots we set off for Coniston.

It was only a short drive, being out of season and quiet.

'In the summer', Amanda said, 'the roads were usually crowded with holiday makers, and it would take twice as long'.

For the same reason the car park at Coniston Pier only contained a few cars. The ferry took us down Coniston Water to a jetty on the eastern side near to the southern end. We talked about Coniston Water being the place where Donald Campbell set many water speed records. He crashed and met his untimely death in 1967 travelling more than 300 mph and is still down there beneath the water with his boat Bluebird. On a lighter note, Amanda talked about some islands in the lake where Arthur Ransome based his children's book Swallows and Amazons, which had passed me by.

Leaving the jetty, we turned left, following the lane to the car park at Dodgson Wood and took the exit. It was tranquil walking through the delightful woodland with the crunch of the autumn leaves under foot. We continued past a barn on the left before starting the stiff climb up the lakeside then over stiles and becks to Low Parkamoor Farm. After the farm it was fields and grassy paths then a gate with a stony path uphill again that had my legs aching on the steady climb. At one point we had to step to the side as a group of mountain bikers came zooming down.

Stunning views appeared as we went over the crest of the hill, I had to stop and take a photograph; then down a slight descent to a viewpoint, where we sat on the grassy ledge. It was a magical spot over-looking the lake to have our picnic. We sat for quite a long time in silence enjoying each other's company watching the boats going back and forth like water beetles.

'That looks so idyllic,' Amanda said pointing across the lake to where a shepherd was rounding up a flock of sheep. Those dogs are so clever it must take a lot of dedication to train them.

'Do you have a dog?'

'No', she replied 'I like them but like children, I prefer other peoples. I like to see dogs working with people, a guide dog or a policeman and I can understand some people needing a companion, but I don't have the patience to train one. Having an animal is too much of a tie; it's worse than having a baby. You must be up early to let it out or feed it. If you go away and take it with you there are so many places you can't go or stay. At least with a baby you can go to a restaurant, cinema or even the zoo with a pet you can't. I would love to have been an aunt taking a niece or nephew to the zoo, then bringing them back so I could get on with my life. I think I am too selfish. I felt dreadfully sorry for Agnes when Chang died. I was hoping she would have children that I could spoil'.

'Chang,' I asked?

'Chang was born in China', she said. 'They met at the Chinese Circus School in Manchester where he had come to teach acrobatics. When he was a young boy in China he just wanted to belong, so he joined the local gang. The problem was it was the Red Dragon Tong and once you're a tong member you're a member for life. They wanted him to spy on the Professor but when he refused, they killed him. No one refuses an order from the Tong. So now she just wants to enjoy life and forget. She uses sex as a painkiller, if she fancies someone that's enough. Like you and Agnes in Lincoln that time.'

I obviously blushed for she hurried on saying, 'don't concern yourself Agnes and I have no secrets, and I am glad you were able to make her happy even if it was just for a short time. I couldn't do that; have sex just for the physical gratification. I would have to love someone deeply before I could give myself.'

It was then I told her my life story. Helen and the boys. Read & Son and all those customers. How life is a bastard, and some people seem to get all the luck and others, well you know. Just go to any hospital and you will see the unlucky ones, the blind and the disabled, perhaps seeing life from a wheelchair while others don't see them at all.'

'Michael died just along there', said Amanda quietly.

'Michael,' I asked?

'Michael was my fiancé. That's his coat your wearing', she said.

'You don't have to tell me', I said.

'I want to. You're the first person I feel able to talk to since the accident'.

'You see we used to come up to the boat most weekends and mountain bike through these hills. It was very exhilarating. Climbing up one side then soaring down the other. In a day we would travel miles, we were fit and hadn't a care in the world until that last day when coming down a track too fast Michael hit a tree root and went over the handlebars. We called out the mountain rescue and the helicopter but to no avail. He had broken his neck and died on the way to hospital. That was a week before the wedding and I haven't been on a bike since', she said.

'We had everything, love, dreams, and a home, neither of us wanted children because we had each other and our careers. Michael was a doctor, a surgeon soon to be a consultant and I helped my father, the Professor. I still have that, but it has paled. I want to go off somewhere exotic like the Virgin Islands and live on a beach and let the whole sorry mess of a world pass me by; I just need to win the lottery.'

I didn't know what to say, so said nothing. After a while Amanda sighed, getting up packing up the remains of our lunch and we continued our walk. Coming down that steep path was absolute agony. The muscles on my shins were on fire as I staggered down. Amanda began to laugh and continued until we were both sitting there laughing together. It was a sort of relief letting out the sadness in our lives. Bikers passed us by looking at us as if we were mad. Back on level ground my legs returned to a usable state as we walked slowly along the lakeside in the dusk. It just seemed natural that our hands brushed then held as we shared the moment.

The next morning, I had to leave after breakfast to go to the factory. I grasped the Professor's hand thanking him for his hospitality.

Turning, Amanda kissed my cheek and impulsively I asked if she would care to go to the Free Trade Hall in Manchester the following week. The Halle Orchestra were playing Tchaikovsky's 5th symphony, and we could have dinner afterwards. Her face was beautiful as she smiled and willingly agreed.

I collected Amanda from their home in Uppermill on the outskirts of Oldham. From outside the Professor's house looked dark and forbidding being built of solid stone blocks. However, as soon as the door opened, light flooded out together with music and warmth from a log fire. While waiting for Amanda the Professor was telling me that the village was one of a group of seven that formed 'Saddleworth' and was formally part of Yorkshire, until it was hived off to be part of Lancashire then Greater Manchester. History is so complex with feuds and wars, and you never knew who had been in the right as history is always written by the winners. Some of the older residents still considered themselves Yorkists and not Lancastrians it seems the Wars of the Roses are not over after nearly 500 years.

The Professor went on to explain that the house had previously been four weaver's cottages where the families lived downstairs while the top floor was taken over by looms. It was a truly cottage industry until the industrial revolution, when the big mills where built and large power-driven looms installed. It had been a time of great civil unrest with home workers breaking into the mills and smashing the looms as their way of life as well as their livelihood disappeared. The Professor had purchased the cottages just after they had been converted into a single house.

The Free Trade Hall had a long history; the most well-known part being Winston Churchill's speeches when he was MP for Oldham.

During the first half of the evening, they played a variety of different pieces ending with a Viola solo. Now, the Viola is a great instrument and, in an orchestra, adds a rich mellowness to the strings but as a solo instrument it was a mournful dirge. Well, this one was. Everyone was fidgeting wishing he would finish but it seemed the more we fidgeted the stronger he played. At last, he ended, and we headed for the bar. A riot of noise and colour as everyone jostled trying to find the interval drinks, they had ordered. Finding ours we managed to get in the corner for some privacy while the world swirled past us. Comments floated in the air, 'That solo went on a bit'. 'I only came to hear the 5th'. 'Is that a new dress you're wearing?' 'Where's my drink?' None of it mattered, didn't touch us as we stood there sipping our drinks our auras mingling, communicating without words. The second half of the concert was the 5th. Sitting there holding hands, the music washing over and around us. We were lost in world of sound and feeling that must be experienced to be appreciated.

We drove back through Manchester's lonely streets in silence, just being with each other, looking out at the flotsam of life. The late-night revellers staggering home in their alcohol induced haze. The sound of an ambulance or police car hurrying to an emergency. It all added to our feeling of well-being; 'love' if you like.

Over the next six months Amanda was often away doing something for the Professor. She said she couldn't tell me what she had been doing or where she had been. She wouldn't even confirm that she had been in this country. I approached the Professor, but he wouldn't tell me, saying, 'It could jeopardise her safety and I should not press her on the matter'. No wonder Amanda wanted to get away from the Professor's work.

We met every two or three weeks either for dinner somewhere or just the cinema to see the latest blockbuster. However, I felt our relationship had progressed to a point when with trepidation I asked her to come away for a walking weekend in the Peak District. Time seemed to stand still for Amanda said nothing, just looked at me with those searching eyes as if she could read my soul.

'Yes', she said at last. That one word said so seriously had my heart in a vice.

'Single rooms of course', I stammered, 'there's a nice B & B in Edale, near the start of the Pennine Way with lots of good walks.'

'No', she said, 'book a double room'.

To save time we decided to meet at Edale early the following Saturday booking in at the B & B and we walked. We walked all morning stopping off at the 'Hut', a converted railway goods wagon; a haven for walkers with bacon rolls and large mugs of tea for lunch. By the time we got back to Edale the pub was serving early dinner, and we sat amongst the other walkers in a sort of camaraderie of fellow enthusiasts. Being late September the nights were drawing in, so we walked slowly hand in hand in the late evening to the B & B.

As we entered the room Amanda turned and kissed me, not the passionate kiss I was hoping for but something quite sisterly.

'I'll go to the bathroom first, shall I?' she said, as the door closed behind her. Some 20 agonising minutes later she appeared wrapped in a large white towel saying, 'Your turn'.

I had the fastest shower of my life, wrapped a towel around my waist and went into the bedroom to find Amanda lying on the bed, the crisp white sheet right up to her chin. 'Turn the light out and open the curtains,' she said.

I did so and climbed in bed beside her.

'Take me,' she said, 'do what you want with me.' I could only imagine her beauty; she was as sexless as a Barbie doll. Instead, I looked at her face in the last of the twilight.

'Don't you want me,' she cried? 'Am I not attractive?'

'You're the most beautiful woman I have ever met,' I said.

'So why don't you want me?' she repeated with a sob.

'That's just it; I do want you very much, but I don't want to just have you. I want us to make love; I want us to enjoy each other; I want us to have pleasure together; to give each other pleasure; to join our bodies together in the most intimate way.'

'But I want to give myself to you,' she said, 'I don't understand what you mean', turning her head away from me.

I gently kissed a line from her shoulder to her ear, which I gently nibbled; she sighed and leaned against me. She smelt of a woman in her prime, that indiscernible mix of pheromones from a woman's skin with a hint of Dolca Vita, the perfume she always wore.

Amanda turned in my arms and looked for a long moment into my eyes. I kissed her gently a soft lingering kiss, her lips softened from a hard thin line until she started to return the kiss, as I slowly lowered the sheet, she became tense. Raising her head slightly I kissed her throat tracing a line to the valley of her breasts, then each breast. I continued kissing her, down over that flat belly and navel to a light fluffy down of hair. 'What are you do.........oh?

We lay together in that afterglow of love making until I heard Amanda crying.

'What's the matter,' I asked tenderly?

'I didn't know I could feel like that, it was the most wondrous feeling I have ever had. The nuns at the convent said the pleasures of the flesh were evil, as were men. Women should be ashamed of their naked bodies and not demean themselves in front of men. Women just had to give themselves so they could have children and take no pleasure themselves. It was our fate ever since Eve took the apple in the Garden of Eden, no more. They were wrong. How could anything as wonderful as we have experienced together be wrong.'

'I love...........', I began. Amanda stopped me by placing a figure on my lips saying 'Don't say it. I want you to tell me you love me when your whole being loves me, when you can't live without me. Not when you may be saying it as you think it's the right thing to do.'

We made love twice more that night. At least Amanda did not have a mother to fill her head full of taboos but also, she did not have someone to teach her the ways of pleasure. However, Amanda was a willing pupil and thanks to Agnes I was a willing teacher.

Then a month later the news that had me feeling sick. The Professor was taking the family back to Hong Kong for a three-month holiday before it was handed over to the Chinese in 1997.

They would be visiting Ju's only relative her younger sister Li and their old home for one last nostalgic visit; just in case there were any travel restrictions once the Chinese re-took possession. Apart from the sightseeing a lot of the time would be spent at the racetrack as Li's husband was one of the top jockeys in Hong Kong.

Amanda insisted that I should not say goodbye at the airport but the day before; saying that they wouldn't have any time alone together.

Three months without Amanda. Three months of going back to the drudgery. Three months of that empty house. Three months of loneliness. Three months of celibacy. I felt sick to my stomach.

Chapter 5

At last Amanda came home.

'Next month', Amanda said, 'there's a ball at the Midland Hotel in Manchester for a charity I support. You know the type of thing. Black tie, dinner, a bit of dancing. I would like to go but I can't go alone so will you escort me?'

'That's a very old-fashioned expression but yes I would love to', I replied.

'There will be lot of a wine, so I better book us in at the hotel to stay the night', she said. 'It will have to be two singles as there are a lot of eyes about and in those circles, I have to think about my reputation', she said.

'Of course,' I agreed reluctantly.

On the day of the ball, I collected Amanda and drove to the Midland.

'It's one of those grand hotels from the age of steam; distinct in its orange and white brick,' she said. 'In its heyday it was *the* place to be. It was the first place in Britain the Tango was demonstrated and was a home for great 'blues' players of the time as well as celebrities such as Mr Rolls and Mr Royce. Where the steps are now into the foyer the carriages used to draw in under the arch so the passengers could alight in the dry. They would stay in opulence and perhaps eat, as you can today, in the 'French' restaurant with its own five chefs who cook for no other guests. When ready to depart they could walk along a covered walkway direct to the station that has now become the GMEX.

We arrived at the entrance to be greeted by a liveried doorman in a top hat who whistled up staff to take our baggage and park my car. The doorman ushered us through the revolving door telling me that my car would be waiting for me when I wanted to leave. The foyer certainly makes a statement with its cream and gold plasterwork everywhere and black marble columns stretching to the high ceiling. We approached the reception to the right to be greeted by 'Hanna', as her name plate stated, and asked how she could help. After stating our names and we had reservations for two single rooms 'Hanna' looked a little nervous as she informed us that due to the ball, they only had one single room left as there had been an accident in a single room that morning making it uninhabitable. The duty manager must have sensed something was wrong, as he came over asking what the problem was, which was quickly explained.

'Hanna, what rooms do we have available?' he asked.

'Only the Master Suite', she replied.

'Then the lady shall have that, at no extra charge of course' he said.

'The Master Suite', we asked?'

Looking up Hanna said, 'It's the room the Prime Minister has when they have the Party conference at GMEX'.

'That's it, Miss Gilmore is in the Master Suite and Mr Read is in 617', she said giving the keys to the porter who had our cases. The porter led us to the lift and up to the 4th floor turning right to the Master Suite. I could not resist having a look at the room, which had a hall with three doors. To the left was a sitting room with a conference/dining table with six chairs and an area of lounge chairs in front of a large TV. The second door revealed a plush bathroom that the porter explained had both a bath and a shower cubicle. 'The only room in the hotel that had both', he said. Going back into the hall the porter led us through into the bedroom that contained a very large bed that only took up half the large room. Opposite was another large TV next to a dressing table and to the right of that facing the door a full-length mirror that was almost three feet wide. Turning Amanda whispered, 'you know how to spoil a girl'.

'I'll collect you at 7.30', I said, giving her a kiss on the cheek. Leaving Amanda, we continued to the 6th floor to my normal hotel size single. It had all the usual amenities, but I must admit it was a disappointment after the 'Master' Suite. I killed a couple of hours by watching the TV then after a shower and a shave I was ready to collect Amanda in dinner jacket and black tie. Rather than use the lift I walked down the wide stairs with its wrought iron balustrade and ornate wallpaper.

Standing in front of the door to Amanda's room I was a little nervous as I knocked but as I did it swung in not closed properly. Stepping into the small hallway I knocked on the bedroom door and hearing Amanda's 'Come in Joe' I entered to see a vision in gold.

'Wow', I exclaimed.

Amanda was standing in front of that full length mirror, looking at her reflection. Her blond hair was piled high exposing her long slender neck above a gold lama dress that reached down to the floor. The dress was backless, stopping just above that round peach of a bottom with the front held up by two thin straps. Four small spotlights trained on her from the ceiling making her glow from top to toe.

Pirouetting to face me she spread her slender brown arms wide saying, 'I'm ready' and picking up a small gold clutch bag headed for the door. Outside she held up her little bag and handed me her door key saying, 'I only have room for a lipstick and a tissue'. Pocketing the key we walked to the lift, her arm in mine my heart pounding in my chest trying to burst out.

Amanda's entrance to the ballroom was nothing less than spectacular. The ceiling was quite low and festooned with pleated material down the walls and from the walls to a central chandelier glowing with multiple bulbs giving an overall sparkling light. At the far end was a raised dais with a band playing behind a small, polished dance floor. Surrounding this were round tables for four, six or eight people each with a six branched candelabra. The gleaming white table linen shone with silver cutlery and pure white table wear.

Most of the tables were already occupied with chattering people nearly drowning the music. The 'maître d'' asked for our invitations then quickly led us to our table. When I say led, I meant he went to our table and stood behind Amanda's chair. Amanda on the other hand glided across the room with every man's eye following her and many of the women's. The men's eyes turning to me as if to say; why couldn't it be me with that beautiful woman instead of that ordinary looking Joe. The women's glances were of shear envy.

Amanda's personality was on fire as she talked to the other couples at the table. One, a GP and his wife, who of course had a horse; the other a boring banker who tried all evening to sell me a pension; with a wife who seemed to spend all her life lunching with friends and name dropping. The meal was very good considering the number of people the hotel was catering for. The starter was the usual prawn cocktail but generous and well presented with a choice of two main courses and two sweets. Cheese and biscuits to follow and coffee preempted the inevitable speeches about the charity. It seemed it had done very well this year but always needed more money so an auction would follow. The auction seemed to go on forever, as the auctioneer was some TV celebrity or other who hammed it up. I bought Amanda some gold earrings at an inflated price, which pleased her.

At last, they were over, the lights dimmed, and the band played. The dance floor quickly filled and saying, 'Excuse us', I took Amanda's hand and led her to the dance floor. I never understood the modern trend for dancing side by side when you could have a woman in your arms with your bodies touching at the hip. Amanda was not satisfied with this as she moulded our bodies together and our cheeks touched as we swayed to the music. My right hand was in the small of her back as we danced. The feel of her warm smooth velvety skin was electric, I gently rubbed my hand up and down her spine intensifying the feeling for us both as Amanda pressed her body harder into mine. It was as if all the other dancers disappeared, and we were in a world of our own wrapped in emotion.

The evening ended as the band played the last waltz. Saying good night to our fellow diners we walked slowly together to the lift then down the corridor to Amanda's room. Stopping outside her door I took out the key unlocking the door. Holding out the key to Amanda I stepped back but instead of taking it she took my hand and led me into the bedroom.

Leaving me just inside the bedroom door she walked to the mirror, her high heels made her sway and her whole body undulated with her bottom naturally swinging to and fro. Stopping in front of the full-length mirror under those spotlights she removed each earing in turn bending over to place each one slowly on the dressing table. The dress pulled so tight across her round bottom it took my breath away as she looked at my reflection with a smile of knowing satisfaction.

Standing she reached up slowly slipping off one strap then the other and the dress shimmered to the floor to reveal her body in its naked perfection. Amanda was one of those lucky women who didn't need a bra. Her breasts where firm mounds of womanhood tipped by small pale pink nipples.

Walking up behind her I put my arms around her waist sliding my hands up to cup her breasts while looking at her magnificence in the mirror. My forefingers touched her nipples rolling them round and round so they swelled and darkened until they looked like exotic pink coral. I kissed her from shoulder to ear along that slender neck as she pressed her bottom into my groin. Spinning in my arms she turned towards me raising her arms around my neck and kissed me. It was long and luxurious I thought my head would explode; I had never been kissed like that before. 'What…..,' I started to ask?

'Ssh,' she said, 'I'll tell you later, just enjoy'.

Taking my hand, she led me to the bed saying, 'Let's make love like we have never made love before'. I cannot put into words how I felt; it was the most significant time of my life.

We lay together in silence not wanting to end the wonderful feeling of joy and satisfaction until Amanda said, 'It was you who said that Agnes had taught you all those things. I talked to her when we were in Hong Kong, and she told me about love and sex. How a man is turned on by what he sees and how a woman should use the Wow factor. I wanted to please you so much I persuaded her to teach me.'

Laughing happily, I pulled her close saying, 'I love you.'

'Take me away from here', she whispered in my ear, 'somewhere exotic. There's a house for sale on St Kitts at Turtle Beach, overlooking the sea they want £1½ m for and it's worth every penny. We can lie on the beach and make love every day'.

'Where was I going to get that sort of money?' I thought.

'What's the problem?' asked the Professor. We were sitting in the Professor's study; the wood fire crackled making a warm atmosphere as Amanda and I sat opposite the Professor who was at his desk, his pipe discarded on the blotter in front of him.

'Joe and I want to live together somewhere warm and exotic', Amanda said, 'but you know his situation'.

After some deliberation the Professor said, 'I suggest to you that we act on your gift voucher plan,' he said.

'We?' I asked. 'Why would you want to do that? You're a man of the law, ex-police and a Professor of Criminology, respected by your peers'.

'You're right but I have been tempted many times to bend the rules to achieve a goal.

What you may find hard to understand is that I chair 'The Council' it's a sort of ACAS[8] for criminal gangs,' he said. 'It's made up of the heads of the criminal gangs where we sort out disputes before they get violent. It keeps the peace and is one reason we have not had any serious turf wars recently with innocent bystanders being injured or killed. They pay me for this service, which is why I can afford the boat.

'I would have thought that gangs wouldn't compromise unless you had some teeth and what stops them strong-arming you by threatening your family?' I asked.

'The Shadow', he said.

'Who or what is the Shadow?' I asked.

---

[8] Advisory, Conciliation and Arbitration Service

Chapter 6

'I'll have to call him something, I'll call him Captain Jones,' the professor began.

He could blend into any landscape be it Columbian Rain Forest or Urban Jungle. He could be the person standing next to you or behind you; that was the fear you had if you thought he was on your trail. What was true was that he was an artist of disguise; you knew he was around, but you never saw him.

He could have been a top professional golfer. His father was the Professional at an exclusive Country Golf Club where he often worked as a caddy for the rich members when he was a boy. Seemingly born with a club in his hand it was golf that taught him self-control, to block out every distraction and make that final putt to win. Fanatical about fitness, each morning he would rise early and run around the course before going to school. In the holidays he would earn his pocket money by working with the green keepers, raking the sand smooth in the bunkers. The youngest ever captain of the junior team, he went on to be a first-class golfer and his father dreamed of him becoming World Number One, but golf was not his ambition; he wanted to be a soldier.

I met Captain Jones some years ago when I was on secondment in Columbia from the UK police to the

Columbian Police as liaison in a combined operation between the CIA[9], CDEA[10] and MI6. The SAS were also on secondment from the MoD helping the Columbian military on rotation with the American Rangers; a combined operation to tackle the drug cartels. The whole thing was being seen as an exercise for future combined British/American deployment aiming to find and iron out any communication or command structure problems.

The SAS/Rangers did deep penetration; identifying key personnel and tracking shipments; I was based at CDEA HQ as communications officer. The problem was timing. The SAS info took too long to reach us at HQ by which time it was often too late for the military to deploy and take effective action.

We decided to move the HQ up country to be closer to the action and improve the response time. The Drug Barons must have had a mole at HQ because they were waiting for us. The convoy consisted of a jeep front and rear, each with four Columbian military soldiers and a high mounted heavy calibre machine gun. I was in a jeep with the military Major liaison officer and a senior CDEA agent behind the lead jeep, closely followed by a truck containing our equipment.

---

[9] Central Intelligence Agency
[10] Columbian Drug Enforcement Agency

We were only half a mile from the forward position and feeling we had made it without incident when they ambushed us. It was a single lane track that had been cut through the Rain Forest by loggers, and it was one of their abandoned camps we were going to use. It was on top of a hill and the forward jeep had gone on ahead to check the road when they hit us as we ground slowly up. There was a loud explosion, and a great tree came crashing down in front cutting us off from the forward party while a fusillade of automatic weapons followed by a hand grenade took out the rear guards in their jeep; not giving them time to return fire.

Our jeep was surrounded by Kalashnikov carrying men who seemed to erupt from the undergrowth giving us no option but surrender. We were dragged out, the Major, the CDEA agent and the driver summarily executed at the side of the road. I was terrified expecting to be next but was dragged back past the truck with its dead driver and the fiercely burning jeep as an ammunition box exploded. The shock wave blew us into the ditch at the roadside where I laid covered in foul smelling slime and water. The body that lay on top of me was dragged off and it was then I saw he had taken the force of the explosion and how I had survived.

After making sure I was not injured I was bundled into the back of a long-wheel-based Land Rover that had backed up fast to the rear of the convoy. It was covered in so much mud that had dried to every shade it was as effective as camouflage paint. It did not have the normal back as there was no access to the driver it was just a metal box bolted on the chassis. A single door in the middle of the rear allowed us access to the bench seats that ran down both sides and there was a single grill for ventilation at the front but no windows. A very large muscular native Columbian followed me and sat at the rear, his back against one wall and his legs across the door with his feet jammed against the other side wall. It was better than any lock as he sat there staring at me with an AK47 cradled across his chest.

Another reason for him jamming himself against the walls of the steel box became apparent as we hurtled back down the track, and I was thrown from one side to the other. I tried to copy my companion, but my feet only just reached the bench seats so had to hang on to the overhead grab rail with both hands to prevent my brains being plastered over the walls as the Land Rover bumped over hardened ruts and swerved back and forth.

It went on for hours; I was covered in bruises, my arms aching intolerably. The air vent at the front of the box did little to help alleviate the smell of my companion who obviously didn't bother with washing. The air got hotter and staler, and I thought I would vomit.

Then it stopped. I heard the driver get out slamming his door and walk to the back opening the rear door. You could not imagine the delight as my companion unwound himself getting out and the fresh air flooding in; I just hung there savouring it.

A hand appeared in the door gesturing forcibly that I should get out. Unlocking my fingers from the rail I crawled to the door where I was dragged out falling to the ground. Looking up I saw a low building, a typical logging camp for the workers. Getting a kick in the ribs I got up and staggered between the two men to the building's single door only to be pushed into a small room with a single metal bed and grass paillasse, a dirty hand basin and a bucket. Light filtered onto the dirt floor through a single barred window high up on the far wall. All this I saw briefly as the door slammed shut behind me and a bolt shot home.

The brackish warm water from the single tap slacked my thirst but did nothing to revive me as I flopped onto the bed falling instantly asleep.

It was dark when I awoke to the noise of the bolt being pulled back and the door opening; my companion of earlier came in gesturing to the open door and going through it found the driver, also in jungle fatigues, pointing to another door.

The man who confronted me was nothing special the only difference between him and his companions was that he was not a native but of mixed blood.

'Good evening,' he said in heavily accented English. 'You are probably wondering why you are not also dead at the side of the road. We know who you are, and we know about your military men in the forest who are hunting us, even if we never see them. It was to stop them we kidnapped you and to obtain a ransom for you from your government. You will be kept here with these two men until that ransom is paid. There is no point in speaking to them, they do not understand English just their native tongue. There is no point in trying to escape for where would you go, there is only the forest? We would hunt you down or you would die or both. Do not hope for rescue, no one knows where you are.

You will be fed, and you will have exercise. I will leave you with washing and shaving things. We want you to be fit and healthy when we hand you over as you are worth much money to us alive, dead you are worthless.

I am now going to send the ransom note, so pray your government pays promptly. We have kidnapped many Americans in the past and their people pay well to get them back. It is a good business. Yes?

I need the ring from your little finger.'

'This was my first wife's I have never been parted from it.'

'If you do not give me the ring I will take your finger with it. I need to send it with the ransom note to prove we have you. When the ransom is paid, and you are freed you will be reunited with it. If it is not paid, you will be reunited with your first wife and not need the ring. It is your choice.

Thank you most sensible,' he said.

'I will also leave you some books as you are the first Englishman we have kidnapped your government will probably be slow and want to negotiate, so you may have a long wait.'

The man nodded to one of the men and I was led by the arm back to that room I was going to know well; too well. I could not tell him the British and American governments do not pay ransom on principal as it could encourage others to kidnap their citizens. The ransoms they had been paid in the past were from American businesses who promised their staff they would always pay a ransom for them. If they didn't, they would never get anyone to work in South America. I laid there thinking about being a prisoner and the shit I was in, up to my neck.

The ransom note was delivered to the British Embassy two days later and passed to the embassy's resident IO[11] who was directly involved with the counter drugs operation. The ring he placed in the diplomatic bag for London and verification. The

[11] Intelligence Officer

note was photocopied and the original passed to CDEA and the Columbian Police for forensic analysis.

To the British Government

We have your policeman he is in good health he will remain so until you pay the ransom which is in two parts.

1.   Remove your military men from the forest and take them back to Britain. Leave Columbian matters to Columbians.

2. $1,000,000 US dollars to be paid where and when we say.

Agree to these terms by placing an advertisement in the personal column of the *El Tiempo* newspaper saying, 'Lucy is going Home.'

To prove we have your man his ring is enclosed. He says it belonged to his first wife.

If you do not agree we will shoot him in the leg and leave him in the forest for the Jaguars. It will not be a quick or pleasant death.

Signed El Baron

Captain Jones was informed of the note's contents by the IO. His orders were to withdraw his men from the field and do nothing until the ring had been verified and instructions received from London.

Within 48 hrs a reply came from London verifying the ring and an "Add" placed in the El Tiempo personal column. It read 'Lucy wants to talk'.

'Isn't that dangerous,' asked Captain Jones.?

'The alternative is to tell them we will not pay under any circumstances, and they will kill him,' said the IO. 'They will not kill him while they believe we may give in, perhaps for a lower ransom. This is playing for time until we find a location. Then you can take your men in.'

Despite there being no hope of escape my army training took over for I had to keep fit ready for the opportunity if it ever came. Not too, was to give up and that was not in my nature. I first had to give my captors names so I could structure my thoughts. In the end I named them after the tunnels in 'The Great Escape' Tom, Dick and Harry; it was rather juvenile, but they made me smile every time I used them.

Each morning, I arose from that lumpy paillasse, stretch exercised to get the kinks out and strip washed. Breakfast always came about 0800 hrs with lunch at 1300 hrs and the evening meal 1900 hrs. It was the same food every time, a sort of stew with lumps of unrecognisable meat and hunk of 'Arepa' maize bread. Each afternoon about 1700 hrs I was taken to the front yard and allowed to exercise for an hour while Dick and Harry watched from each end: their guns on clear display across their chests.

Things to pass the time were limited. I drew a calendar on the wall behind the door so the guards wouldn't see it. The books were varied including a Holy Bible inscribed 'Left by the Gideon Society at the Hollywood Downtowner Inn in Los Angeles' and a copy of 'The Count of Monti Cristo'; Tom really had a sadistic sense of humour.

Tom came back after three days. I only knew when Dick opened the door but instead of bringing in the evening meal pointed to the door. Tom's door was open, and I heard him call, 'Come in'.

'I thought you might like some conversation with your meal,' he said, pointing to a table with two chairs. It certainly wasn't The Ritz but certainly better than sitting on the bed.

'The ransom note has been delivered, now we wait for their reply.'

'How long,' I asked?

'I should think about a week maybe two; you're not tiring of our company already,' he laughed?

I was pleased that he ate the same meal as I had been forced to eat. It must have been their staple diet.

As Harry took the plates away Tom said, 'Do you play Cribbage?'

'Cribbage?'

'Cribbage the card game.'

'Yes, I know what it is and yes, I do play. Most soldiers do; it helps to fill the time when you are waiting for something to happen.'

'Good. These men are fine for guarding but short on conversation. My father taught me the game, and we played many times.'

Each time Tom came back from wherever he went we ate together, played Cribbage and drank some fiery spirit until the small hours.

It had been three months since the kidnapping and finally they had a location. It was certainly remote, the nearest they could get was a rocky outcrop 50 miles from the camp. The extraction LZ where a helicopter could land was 80 miles in the opposite direction.

Captain Jones decided to take just his Sergeant on the operation.

'Wouldn't it be better with more men?' queried the Sergeant.

'If it comes to a fire fight the first thing they will do is kill their prisoner. This needs to be a surgical strike, that way we get the prisoner unharmed and then run like hell for the LZ with the Columbian drug gang hunting us. I hope Gilmore is in shape and knows how to take orders.'

They went in by Columbian Air Force helicopter abseiling on to the rocky outcrop and it took them three days to get close enough to set up an OP[12].

---

[12] Observation post

They observed two men coming and going around the building then at 1700 hrs the prisoner emerged. The two men positioned themselves: one at each end of the yard, AK47's covering the yard. The prisoner started by marching twice round the yard and then jogged twice round, then twice at a full run only to drop when he was level with the door and did ten press-ups. Then he did it over and over for a full hour, until the guards called a halt, and they went inside.

'No worries about him being in shape, he reminds me of my Drill Sergeant at Sandhurst,' said the Capt. as they lay side by side. 'Did you see his uniform, clean and pressed and he marched round that yard like he had a ramrod stuck up his jacksie.'

A third man arrived about 1900 hrs in a very dirty Land Rover, went inside and one of the other men came out and unloaded two boxes taking them inside. There was no further movement that night.

The man from the Land Rover left about 1000 hrs the next morning and the routine continued for another three days until the land Rover returned.

'There doesn't seem to be anyone else around. If the man in the Land Rover leaves tomorrow as last time we'll take him at exercise tomorrow night,' they agreed.

They lay side by side in their hide, deep in the shadows of the forest. Anyone walking within a few feet of them wouldn't have seen them; they were concealed by camouflage netting from the tips of their boots to the tips of their rifles.

'We'll fire just as he drops to do press-ups after the first cycle, the guards will be looking at him. Head shots both at the same time; we don't want them wounded, spraying bullets around.'

The morning started like every other. My uniform was pressed from being under the paillasse all night followed by the usual stew for breakfast. I had read all the novels twice, before I started reading the bible. I had never realised that there were so many interesting stories of love, courage, betrayal and murder in the Old Testament; it was a really good read. The only change was Tom had been very angry the night before.

'Over three months. They talk and talk. I have compromised. I agreed to reduce the ransom to $500,000 and they still won't pay. Need more time they say. Well, no more time. If they don't pay now, I'll send you back in bits.' There was no Cribbage that night.

I looked forward every day to exercise time; it took my mind off my situation, if only briefly. Each day I tried to go faster pitting myself against time as I had nothing else to compete against.

It happened just as I completed the first run and dropped down to start the press-ups. A rifle shot with what sounded like an instant echo but was in fact two shots, made me drop to the ground and freeze. Turning my head, I saw both Dick and Harry were lying in crumpled heaps near where they had been standing guard. It was then, what looked like two small trees, walked out of the forest.

They lay in their hide and seeing the third man drive off in the Land Rover got on the radio for a pickup at 1800 hrs not at the LZ but here as there was enough space in the yard and they wouldn't be running for their lives from a hoard of angry men. Everything was set by 1600 hrs. They lay relaxed; their rifles pointing to where the two men would stand; the sergeant's to the left and the Capt.'s to the right. Like clockwork the door opened, and the three men walked out. The guards took up their usual positions while the prisoner began his routine. Round he went and the Capt. said, 'On my count of three'.

'One, two, three'. They fired and the brains of two men were sprayed across the yard.

Some years later we met again by chance at the Union Jack Club, the hotel in London for service personnel of all countries. He was standing looking at the display of VCs from all ages and all wars.

'Captain Jones, I believe.'

Turning he looked down with surprise, 'Assistant Chief Constable I never expected to see you here and it's just Mr Jones.'

'Mr Jones? You have left the army?'

'My wife has been ill for several years and never told me. She didn't want my mind on her when I was on active and make a fatal mistake. She collapsed last year. That's how I found out; it seems it is stress related and me being on active made it worse. I had to make a decision and came out.'

'What are you doing now?'

'Working for the old man at the golf club as Assistant Pro.,' he said. 'I'm taking the PGA teachers exams and should be qualified next year; then the old man plans to retire and let me take over.

Anyway, enough about me what are you doing here?'

'It's a nostalgia trip. I normally stay here when I'm in "London" as I am an Associate Member, being in the police force. I'm retiring next month and will give up my Warrant Card and with it my membership here.'

'I can't imagine you retiring; you're still in your prime.'

'Unfortunately, not in my prime but there are still a few years in me yet. I have been offered an Honorary Professorship of Criminology at Manchester University, but I don't know how I'm going to adjust to not being involved in the action.'

'I feel the same way. Teaching a blue rinsed OAP to putt doesn't compare with the thrill of active service.'

'Let's go and talk somewhere private,' I said.

In a corner of the empty Officers' Dining Room, we sat and talked of organised crime.

'As a policeman there was one problem I could never deal with and that was innocent bystanders getting injured or killed in the gang wars over territory. London is typical; there's a gang based in North London wanting to extend its area. The problem is the area they are moving into is controlled by an established gang based in the East End. It won't be long now before the East End gang has to teach the interloper a lesson. There will be tit-for-tat beatings that will escalate into knifings then the guns come out with bullets flying everywhere.

What they need is some neutral organisation they could go to and negotiate an agreement. Something like 'ACAS' where the unions and bosses meet and thrash out a deal.

So, The Council was conceived. I would do the talking, and he would do the enforcing; and only I would know his identity.

The problem was how to make the gangs take notice and agree to an outsider basically giving orders, let alone someone they would see as police? There had to be a highly visible lesson made by an invisible enforcer before they would accept my judgements and agree a retainer for our services. Also, my position was vulnerable, so we had to be even more ruthless than the criminals or at least appear to be. We agreed to start with the most vicious, the most paranoid egotist of all "London".

"London" lived in an old Victorian house that used to be a convent. It was ideal for his psychotic personality being surrounded by high brick walls topped with broken glass. The old vegetable gardens had been cleared and the whole area around the house was now grass. The only break in that perfect expanse was the gravel drive leading from a heavy wooden gate to the turning circle in front of the house and the only way through that massive wall.

On each corner of the house infrared cameras covered every inch of the ground from the wall to the house and monitored 24/7 by an armed guard in a small room at the back of the house. It was the only time "London" felt safe to sleep without fear of attack by a rival gang or more likely his cousin and number 2 wanting the top job.

Getting over the wall was not a problem for a man of his training; neither were the two Rottweilers that roamed the grounds after dark. From the top of the wall a short blast on a dog whistle had brought them running and now they lay on the grass, each with a small dart protruding from their skin.

The Shadow lowered himself to the grass completely invisible to the cameras thanks to his ex-SAS suit that covered every part of him except for his eyes. It was completely black and looked like a diver's wet suit but was based on the suits used by astronauts doing EVAs. It kept the user cool in the most extreme environment but had the benefit of masking his body heat so that he seemed like a passing shadow to the cameras.

This shadow seemed to glide up the wall via the old cast iron rain pipe until it hovered outside the window of the sleeping man. A small device was attached to the glass, cutting a hole silently and allowing a stream of Nitrous Oxide to fill the room.

The shadow made a larger hole to unlock the window and vented the gas now it had done its work. The figure in the bed was asleep but another dose direct via a facemask made sure he stayed that way until the security guard could be nullified. It ended up being much simpler than expected and needed just a knock on the door for it to be opened by a sleepy guard who mumbled, 'It's ok boss I wasn't asleep', only to be put sound asleep by a carefully aimed blackjack.

With the cameras off and the gates open it was just a matter of driving a small van up to the front door dumping in the sleeping man and leaving a note for the guard. It was not short, but it was to the point.

TELL EVERYONE THAT I HAVE GONE AWAY FOR A COUPLE OF DAYS ON BUSINESS.

IF YOU TELL ANYONE ANYTHING ELSE, I WILL DEAL WITH YOU WHEN I RETURN.

He had a massive headache but didn't know why. He wasn't lying on his bed but something hard angled at about 45°. Opening one painful eye he saw nothing, it was pitch black so opened the other that sent a stab of pain across his forehead. He didn't know where he was. Turning he found he couldn't move more than six inches; his hands and feet were chained to the board. He began to sweat. It must be a bad dream.

There was a noise to he left, and a voice said, 'You're awake'.

'Who are you?' What the fuck is this?' he shouted only to cringe as his head felt like it was going to burst.

'Who am I? You can call me The Shadow'

'The Shadow what's that? You've been reading too many fucking comics. No, you're a dead man. I'm going to kill you.'

'You will find that difficult. You don't know who I am or what I look like.'

'Who sent you?'

'I'm not from any of the other gangs. As to who sent me, you'll find that out in time. First you need to look at something', he said turning on a powerful light over the bed.

The pain in his head was unbearable as he screwed up his eyes against the light. Slowly his eyes adjusted until squinting he could make out a vague shape moving in the darkness beyond the light. A gloved hand appeared holding a photograph.

It was a photograph of him with the cross hairs of a sniper's scope printed in the middle of his forehead.

"London" exploded, 'You bastard you will not live long enough to get out of this building. My men are looking for me now. They will track you down and cut off your balls.'

'Your men are not looking for you. They think you have gone away to a secret meeting, which of course you have.'

'If you kill me, they will come after you.'

'No, they won't; they will be too busy fighting each other about who is going to take over.'

The picture moved away and another replaced it.

It was the picture of a pretty woman kneeling weeding a flowerbed. Beside her a boy of about six holding a blue plastic bucket half full of dandelions and tufts of grass. Each figure also had the cross hairs of a sniper's scope printed on their heads.

'How do you know about them?' he croaked.

'This is to show you that you must take us seriously. I am going to tell you why I was sent but not by whom. He is a well-known figure, and he is the only face you will know. You will never see mine, but I could be at your shoulder at any time. I could have killed you in your sleep, but we have a deal for you that you will find beneficial.'

"London" felt sick. The one thing in this life he cared about was known to this nightmare figure, this Shadow.

'What do you want, money?'

'We'll come to that at the meeting.'

'What fucking meeting?'

'A meeting when the man who sent me will spell out a deal that will benefit all of us.'

'All. What others?'

'You and the heads of the other eight main gangs in Britain and of course my associate.'

'What if I don't want your deal?'

'If you don't want it, you can walk away or you can take the deal then walk away later. If you harm the person who sent me or his family or anyone associated with him at any time, I will revisit you, your son and his mother and I won't have a camera in my hand.

You will be contacted when you will be given a date, a time and a place.

Now I am going to give you an injection to knock you out for a short time. It will be better if you don't struggle, otherwise I may have to hurt you, and we don't want that. Do we?

When you wake, I will be gone, and this place will be clean of any trace of our visit. There is a bag at the end of the bed with a change of clothes and your wallet. Turn left out of the door; there is a taxi rank at the end of the road. I hope we never need to meet again.'

The Shadow visited each of the gangs; in each case photographing the boss, his wife and his children; producing a set of pictures each with the cross hairs. All except one, "Liverpool"; it was his horse and hopeful winner of the next Grand National that was his weak spot.

A month later each received a registered letter delivered to their home. Each had to be at a certain mooring on Windermere at an exact time when a boat would pull in. They were to board alone, go to the rear cabin and take their named place around the table. Once all the bosses had been picked up the boat would anchor in the middle of the mere and they would begin. It took nearly an hour to pick up each one then cruise to an isolated spot where the anchor went out and the engines stopped.

To reduce tension as much as possible the Professor had organised the seating so that old enemies were as far apart as possible with himself at the head as chairman. On his right were "Manchester", "Edinburgh", "Cardiff" and "London". On his left "Glasgow", "Birmingham", "Leeds", "Southampton" and "Liverpool".

The air became charged with static when the "Professor" entered the cabin putting everyone immediately on edge.

'The Filth', spat out "Cardiff".

'Ex-filth; I am now a private citizen,' replied the "Professor".

'Let me first explain this boat is in the middle of the mere and my associate has swept it for bugs. He has also installed a small transmitter on the roof that is sending out 'white' noise so anyone trying to eavesdrop will not be successful. What we say here today will not go any further.

Each one of you has been visited by my associate who you all know as "The Shadow". He has also explained that you may walk away from our proposal without any further action on our part.

However, if you at any time harm me, my family or anything to do with me he will rain retribution on you so bad you will pray for death. He is your worst nightmare. Every time you think you see something out of the corner of your eye you will not be sure if it's a trick of the light or it's him; he will never let you go.

That's enough of that; let's get down to business with an example.'

Turning to "London" he said, 'In your business, what is your biggest headache? Is it your number 2 trying to take over from you or perhaps the "North London" gang muscling in on your area?'

'I can deal with my number 2 but you're right. "North London" is getting too big for his boots and needs a slap but what's that got to do with you?'

'If you teach "North London" a lesson they will retaliate; you will have started a war, and innocent bystanders will be hurt. They are the ones that concern us. It's also bad for business, your profits will drop, and you will spend a fortune on men and guns, and we don't like guns on the streets. It would be much better if "The Shadow" had a chat with him like he has with each one of you around this table and point out the error of his ways. He will then know it will not be his goons that will get hurt in a war, it will be just him. He sticks to his patch, and you stick to yours and everyone's happy.'

'What's in it for you?'

'A retainer; a monthly payment of £5000 from each of you, paid to me and all your inter-gang problems go away.'

'£45,000 a month for doing nothing,' said "Leeds".

'That's right but when you have a problem like "North London" it goes away and costs you nothing. We are only interested in stopping these senseless wars and saving innocents, that's got to be worth a fee and for you it makes good business sense?'

The Council or Criminal Advisory, Conciliation and Arbitration Service was born.

Chapter 7

'You have to think like a criminal to do your job as do I', said the Professor. 'There is a very thin line between a policeman and a criminal; it's a matter of perspective. Some police have been known to use what would be classed as illegal violence to get a confession. Many have received payoffs for turning a blind eye; but each have a line they won't cross. If they do they know there is no way back for they in turn become a criminal. It's a grey area; others would argue that it is very black and white. The temptation is always there, everyone including the most moral person has been tempted at some time. It all comes down to how big the temptation is.

Take this conciliation thing I do. Because I am negotiating with criminals it is a criminal act because I am told what they have done and what the grievance is, I am guilty after the fact if I don't report it to the police. I can't do that otherwise the criminals wouldn't trust me. I justify it by knowing I am saving innocent lives by preventing gang wars. I keep the peace; using the threat of the 'Shadow' is also criminal as were the demonstrations we had to give at the start. But it is the greater good I always wanted. There are certain high-ranking parties in the Home Office who know what I do but turn a blind eye. They are also guilty, so you see it's all a matter of degree.'

'What's changed to make you to want to step over that line?'

'I got old. It's also the size of the temptation you are offering. I think we should get 10% each, that's £6 million; I could be very comfortable for the rest of my life on £6 million.

Look at the criminals I have been chasing. Not the small fry who get caught, the pushers, the burglars but the bosses who sit in their mansions or on their yachts. What do I have to show for all my years? I want to retire with something substantial in the bank, so I don't have to worry but I need your insider knowledge.'

'What you said in your presentation at the conference, were they all lies?'

'No. It was all completely true and it's the only real option to reduce the drug and prostitution problems it's the one legacy I would like to leave. The gangs I work with know it but what they also know is no government will act on it.

You said that one of the main reasons the fraud couldn't take place was getting an army of criminals to pass the vouchers at the same time. We can use a meeting of The Council to put the plan to them and see if for once they will work together.'

Chapter 8

'So, did I want to become a criminal? That went against everything I had done in my life. Yes, I had thought like a criminal and come up with possible ways to defraud organisations but that was just so I could prevent it happening. To commit a crime, it sent shudders through me.

There was Helen and the boys to consider. What would they think? Would they care? Did they need to know? How could I prevent them knowing?

There was Amanda; Beautiful, Gorgeous, Sexy Amanda. Did I want to give her up? Go back to mediocrity? To the job, to Read & Son, to fawning over people I disliked. To being broke as all the money went on horses.

I was scared. I could get caught. I could go to prison!

They were silent just looking at me, reading my thoughts as they went across my face.

'I don't know,' I stammered.

'Think about it darling,' Amanda said, 'we could have that house on St Kitts or wherever you want and be together every day, away from this rat race.'

I went home or what I used to think of as home. It was now just a house where Helen lived. Where was home? I no longer had one. A home was people you loved and who loved you. Helen no longer loved me, and I didn't love her. We did once, many years ago. Then the boys came, and all our focus was on them rather than each other and when they were gone, we had nothing left.

Now there was Amanda. Did I love her, or did she bedazzle me? When I was with her my heart sang and when we parted I felt sick to my stomach. Yes, I loved her. I wanted to be with her I wanted to turn the car around and drive straight back. But to become a criminal!

The house was empty and cold. Cold in the sense it was empty of love, it was a shell, a place to hang one's coat. No wife, no boys, soulless, a place of memories and a note from Helen. She was away to another 3-day event with Sylvia her fellow eventer and friend, back late Sunday and wanting to talk. I couldn't stay in that house, so I went to see my mother.

Dad died 10 years ago, and Mum lived alone in the old family house I grew up in. That house was full of love, for Dad never really died. He still lived on in that house; I could see him all around. Dad was a prolific water-colour artist, there were paintings everywhere. Trees, always trees, in all seasons from bare branches covered in snow to summer in full leaf to autumn in warm browns and gold. He used to say a tree is life in miniature, from nothing to nothing, birth to death. The promise of spring and new life, through summer's brilliance to autumn's withering and winter's death.

I poured out my heart to her. She didn't judge me; she was not that sort of a person; she just listened.

In the end, after I had grown quiet, she asked, 'In your heart, do you love her?'

'My heart says yes but my head says I'm being a fool', I said.

'Life', she said, 'is like a road'. 'We travel along it comfortable in normality and every now and then there is a fork in the road. Do we go left, or do we go right? Do we get a job or go to university; do we marry this person or that; have children or not. They are all forks in the road 'a decision' once you make that decision you can't go back and take the other road. You can only go on to the next. This is one of those forks in the road'.

'What about the boys?

'The boys are no longer boys but grown men with their own lives', Mum said, 'they would say this is your life to live, so live it. Too many people don't make decisions because of their children; they use them as an excuse to avoid reality or difficult situations. They carry on in a miserable job or a bad marriage because it's easy. Easier than making a decision and the consequences they will have to live with. They are scared'.

'Can I stay here? I asked.

'Of course, your old room is still there, it's not a place to hide from the world but if you want somewhere to think.'

'Thanks Mum that's what I need; somewhere to think'.

That weekend was like the eye of a hurricane. We walked together in the garden, mum showing me an arbour she had had made so she could sit and talk to Dad. Trimming a hedge that had grown too tall; picking vegetables for dinner. We ate together, sitting on the veranda, drank wine and watched the Sun go down. Mum was right, I had been hiding but I had made a decision.

It was Sunday evening; Helen would be back, and I had to go back into the world. The house lights were on; Helen was sitting at the kitchen table, the harsh fluorescent light making her skin pale and older than her years; a bottle of Gin at her elbow, looking for courage, to say what?

'Joe, I want a divorce', Helen said.

How on earth had she found out about Amanda or was it my impending criminal career?

I was dumbstruck. My face must have shown my shock.

'I didn't mean to blurt it out like that', she said. 'I'm sorry; it was brutal to just come out with it. It's not your fault. You're a good man but we have separate lives, we have different interests. I talked it over with John when he was last down from Cambridge'.

'You've talked to John', I said.

'He said to do whatever I wanted; it was my life to live and not worry about the boys'.

'Where will you live' I asked?

'Here, we'll buy you out and you can buy a flat. We have another house to sell, and you can take whatever you want, furniture, TV, anything'.

'Do I know him, what's his name,' I asked?

'Sylvia', she said.

'Sylvia; the woman you ride with', I spluttered? 'You mean you're a lesbian?'

'Heavens No,' she said. 'We both came to the conclusion that we prefer horses to men.'

I wanted to tell you earlier, but we had to wait until Sylvia's divorce came through. Now she has the house and the children'.

'Children', I said.

'Yes, two boys, but they spend most of the time at boarding school. Then in the school holidays Sylvia's mother has them when we are away at events. You see we have it all worked out'.

'So that's it,' I said, 'you have it all worked out. What about my feelings, what I want to do?'

'You're never here, she said, 'you don't need a home you need a laundry service. You're always away staying in hotels enjoying yourself. You won't miss me at all.'

She was half right.

Two weeks later I was back at the Professor's house.

'Can we have a chat?' I asked.

'Certainly Joe', he said, 'come into the study. We won't be disturbed in there'.

'I agree, I'll do it,' I said as we sat down.

'Think about it Joe if you go ahead with this you can't change your mind,' he said.

'I've made up my mind, I want Amanda, and I want a life with her without any worries.'

'We will have to call a special full meeting of The Council with all the bosses present and you will have to do a good sales job on them,' he said.

'Me, I can't face them; they're criminals,' I said.

'So will you be if we go ahead with this,' he said. 'Now spell out what we have to do'.

'Produce test prints of all the stores vouchers so we know we can print them to a good enough standard and to have samples to show the gang bosses; convince the gangs to come on board and agree the timescale and the need for secrecy; print

15 million vouchers; distribute and rake in the money. That's all.'

'I can't see how we are going to print the samples let alone 15 million vouchers,' said the "Professor".

'I may have solved that problem', I said.

'I thought of my comment about selling a Rolls Royce and baked beans. As I said we can't use the big printers as the police would soon get wind of it. What we need is whole host of small ones like "Pronto print" or "KopyKat". We can't use them, so we are going to set up our own'.

'That will cost a fortune', he exclaimed.

'That's why we are going to get the government to fund it', I said.

'You're joking'.

'The Home Office have for years struggled to stop prisoners reoffending. They educate them; teach them trades with full qualifications. They even get degrees in Management Studies and the like but as soon as they apply for a job, they must admit they have been in prison. Now if you were an employer and you had two identically qualified candidates for a position and one has been in prison, who would you choose? The one without the criminal record may be a bigger rogue, just never got caught. The ex-prisoner reoffends and ends up back in prison.

I was talking to a junior Home Office Minister, and he had this wonderful idea or was it mine, anyway he believes it was his which I totally agree with. The government sets up a series of businesses with a head office doing the marketing and lots of local companies based on the Franchise system. The main qualification for employment is to be an ex-prisoner or ex-con as the Americans call them. The junior minister told his idea to the senior minister, and he told the Home Secretary now it's his idea and the business is called "ConPrint".

They teach inmates at Leyhill Prison and others to become printers, so it was the obvious choice. Each franchise is to be owned by an ex-prisoner or prisoners and set up as a sole trader, partnership or cooperative. They are to obtain a bank loan and guarantee 50% of the start-up capital from legitimate sources such as their home(s) and the government will guarantee the other 50%. If the business folds the government gets any assets to repay its part of the bank loan. That way all the risk is the ex-con's not the taxpayer and like everyone else starting a new business they have every incentive to make it work. The fact that we have another group of workers using the print machines at night is no one else's business and with twenty of so shops we will have the volume we need.'

'I like your lateral thinking.'

'The Home Office needed someone at head office who they trust. After a great deal of persuasion and personal sacrifice I have agreed to resign as MD of Read & Son and become the MD of ConPrint at a greatly increased salary.

'You crafty bugger.'

'I also chair the selection board for the staff and the franchisees. I will get the files on applicants before the interview boards, and we can go through them; that way we can get the right people involved who will cooperate.

Once we have the first ones set up, we run some trials to make sure they can print what we want at night. We then have our samples to show the 'bosses'; once they're signed up for the scam we start printing; if they don't, nothing lost. The local gangs won't have to do anything except provide secure premises to accept deliveries and break the parcels into small lots for the foot soldiers. That's eighteen months away making our deadline the Christmas after next but before we do all that we need to find out if the gangs would go for it by sounding out just one', I said.

'I know it will increase the risk, but I think it's one we must take. Is there one you can trust to keep his mouth shut?'

'"Manchester" is the obvious one. He and I were at loggerheads for years when I was in the force. We have what you would say a mutual respect,' said the Professor.

'Why do you call him "Manchester" why not his name?

'We don't use names you never know whose listening, no matter what precautions we take. I think we can still refer to you as Joe as it's equally anonymous.'

The Professor set up a meeting on his boat where we met a week later. The Professor and I were there early, waiting with some trepidation as this was the moment when the whole project could fail. He was late, we looked at one another thinking the same thing, he wasn't coming, then a black Range Rover pulled into the car park with a squeal of tyres; "Manchester" had arrived.

I don't know what I was expecting but certainly not the tall, rather elegant, well-dressed businessman that got out of the car.

'Good morning, Professor', he said shaking hands.

'Good morning "Manchester". This is Joe he's the brains behind all this', he said.

Turning to me and shaking hands he said, 'If this idea of yours is on, you might end up a very wealthy man'.

To the driver he said, 'Stay here Rob, I'll be quite safe.'

Then turning to the Professor he said, 'If this is as big as you say the fewer people who know about it the better'.

It took us some time to motor out to a safe distance from the shore where we could moor and go below.

'I will leave it to Joe to explain', said the Professor.

'I outlined the plan as I did to the Professor adding that I estimated that gangs would end up with at least a £50 million, how much the bosses keep is up to them but as most of the foot soldiers will probably be addicts so the bosses will end up with most of it when they buy their next fix'.

'It sounds too good to be true and I have a million questions but go on,' said "Manchester".

I went on to explain about ConPrint at which "Manchester" was amazed at my audacity.

'The gangs are not that organised and getting them to work together could be impossible,' said Manchester. 'The ones in Moss Side in Manchester are based at the Street level and there can be bitter rivalry with the gang in the next street. London has one main gang with one small one.'

'I didn't explain that properly,' I said. 'They don't have to work together just do a single thing at the same time without contacting anyone else. Can they be trusted not to jump the gun and do something precisely as they are told when they are told to do it and how? If one went off on their own, it could mean the slammer for everyone as the police would be waiting for them.'

'That might be possible with the sums of money involved' said "Manchester", 'the bosses will need to impose their rule anyway otherwise vouchers will be leached away, and the shops will be warned.'

'The question is, will the gangs go for it?'

'I think they might but besides me you need to convince the other members, "Edinburgh", "Glasgow", "Leeds", "Cardiff", "Liverpool", "London", "Birmingham" and "Southampton", and for the money you're talking about I think they will, but you have missed one thing; you will need some working capital. I suggest you ask for a non-returnable buy-in of £10,000 each just to show their commitment. That will give you £90,000, including mine, for buying paper, ink and the other bits and bobs you will need as the volumes you will use would stick out in the print shops accounts. Just involve the main gangs as they can maintain order while covering the whole country. Don't involve the smaller ones as they are too loosely organised, and I am sure they couldn't maintain secrecy'.

So, we set to work; I started at ConPrint head office first recruiting a Marketing Director recently released from Holloway and as Chairman a Lord recently convicted of tax evasion that needed money to keep his family pile going while the Professor went round all the stores buying complete sets of their vouchers and gift cards. The Marketing Director was a real find. Margaret Wilkins was serving a custodial sentence for a hit-and-run offence where she killed a cyclist while drugged up to the eyeballs on cocaine or more formally driving under the influence of drugs. Formerly a highflyer in the City, she knew she would never get her position and status back so jumped at the chance we offered.

After discussing our needs, she came up with a two-part plan that meant the shops would offer the usual services of copying, business cards in direct competition with other high street printers. This would not give us the production we needed but establish credibility so the other half of the plan was that each shop would have a high-speed multi-colour press dedicated to printing a single product; A4 colour leaflets.

The plan was centred round TV adverts promising high quality colour leaflets at very low prices; prices so low other printers could not match them. The secret was volume, standardisation and quick turn round. Orders would come in from all over the country to a single order point then brigaded together and farmed out to the various franchises. They could print eight different orders at the same time in multiples of 1000 copies; then cut, pack and despatch. All we had to do was change the printing plate for the next batch using the same paper and ink. This meant that non-production time was kept to a minimum and by running 24 hours a day using the presses to their maximum, keep the costs low. Later they would also offer low-price business cards and letterheads. However, until we went live the night production would be kept free. If the gangs didn't go for the plan they would switch to 24 hr leaflet production.

Chapter 9

The first ConPrint was opened in Norwich accompanied by great fanfare by the Home Office. It was seen as a new step in community involvement in prisoner rehabilitation and crime prevention with the public called on to support the initiative.

The marketing got into full swing with television adds as each new franchise opened. After a month we had ten high street shops each with an offsite factory housing a high-speed multicolour press.

I could have used any of the sites to do the trials but I decided on Manchester so I could see Amanda as much as possible and keep in touch with the Professor. About once a week I joined Brian, the press operator on the night shift. Brian was one of the old school; a lifetime criminal who had spent half his working life in prison and the other half holding up Post Offices. He was the sort of person the Home Office wanted to get on the scheme but would have been shocked if they knew what he was really doing on the night shift.

Meeting Brian the first time was a bit of a shock with his tattooed bald head, broken nose and scarred eyebrows he had a face like a 2nd rate boxer.

'Prison can be a rough place', he said, 'and you don't win all your battles. I ended up in the infirmary more than once.'

However, he knew his stuff for his first reaction was 'How the fuck do you expect me to print all these multi-coloured wavy lines? I can't even begin to imagine how it is done. A red or blue line yes, but one that starts off red then changes to blue and back again across the page. As for the special inks and paper, where are they coming from?'

'I can't explain why but just concentrate on scanning the vouchers and use normal 4-colour process printing and standard inks. Don't worry about the paper that will come later', I said.

'But they will be spotted straight away those lines will be made of dotes like a photograph. Why do you think they print the lines like that? It's so you can't use normal printing', he said, 'and what about the watermarks how are we going to reproduce those.'

'Just do the trials and be ready for the paper. I just want as good a copy as you can do and don't ask any more questions. I would have thought that your time inside would have taught you not to ask questions. Whatever you do, make sure you put every bit of paper and printing plate on the van each night, so the day shift has no idea what you are up to; if you don't it won't be me, you'll answer to.'

Brian was very good and produced a range of samples within two weeks.

'The colours look all false on this white paper. When I am getting the correct paper and I can't do the M&S ones they're just too difficult,' he said.

'I think M&S want them to look like banknotes, so the customers think of them as having a great value and they use the same sort of watermark as banknotes; it's all part of the M&S image. Just rub one gently between your fingers. One side of the watermark is smooth like the other vouchers, but the other feels slightly raised in places. It's what creates all the different shades of grey were the others just have light and dark; as for the paper just hang on.'

'Professor, I've got a problem', I said 'I can't source a paper that will do the job'.

'Can you explain?'

Every paper I can get is bright white, but the UV dead paper is a bit grey, we must get a paper that looks something like it. If I go to a paper manufacturer and order a UV dead paper, they will instantly know what it's for and report the enquiry to the police and no one orders grey paper; that would be equally suspicious.'

'I don't know what the answer, but I think the doctor might be able to help.'

'I'm not ill', I exclaimed.

'Not that sort of doctor. The Doctor, doctors.....Oh hell, he will explain better than I. He lives on a council estate in Fulham where he thinks he blends in'.

Chapter 10

You can lose yourself in Fulham if you don't know it and I didn't. In the end I hailed a taxi and showed the address to the Rastafarian driver.

'Hey man you don't want to go in there; a white man like you. You'll never come out again.'

'I'll have to risk it; I need to see a man.'

'On your own head, be it man; don't tell anyone I didn't warn you.'

He must have had the instincts of a homing pigeon as we wound round the streets until we arrived at a decrepit block of flats.

'Good Luck man', he said and drove quickly away.

If the Doctor was trying to blend in, he was some character. There were used needles and condoms on the staircase and the whole place stank of urine and mould. It should have been condemned years ago rather than left to rot and harbour all sorts of wildlife. The door to the flat looked like it was made of cheap plywood. The paint was peeling to such a degree you could see that at one time it had been green then red and now yellow. There was no letterbox or bell, so I was surprised when I knocked there was not the hollow sound of wood but a dense solid sound of something very thick and strong and metallic. Getting no answer, I knocked again this time using my fist which gave a more substantial booming sound.

'Who are you and what do you want,' barked a voice from a speaker up to my right next to small CCTV camera?

'Are you the Doctor,' I asked?

'Who wants to know?'

'My names Joe, the Professor sent me.'

The voice was obviously convinced as a key turned, and bolts withdrawn. The door opened and a voice said, 'Come in quick, I don't want anyone seeing a honky coming to my door.' There was no light on in the hall and everything was dark as the outer door was closed quickly, and the bolts shot home.

'Just a little home security,' he said laughing.

'In this area I am sure he needs it,' I thought.

I sensed him pass me in the dark then a door opened into a bright modern interior in extreme contrast to outside.

'Welcome to my home,' he said.

'I can see why you need the security, I said. 'You have a nice home, and you like your gadgets'. The latest in television and video equipment was at the end of the room. Next to an open door into a modern fitted kitchen with every labour-saving device you could imagine.

'If I lived in town,' he said, 'my neighbours would say. How could a black man have a home like that he must be a crook? Here I can live like a king in my own domain but to the outside world it is a slum, and no one questions it. People are happy and don't bother me and I don't bother them.'

'The Professor called you 'The Doctor'. The only Doctor I know is 'Doctor Who' and you're certainly not him. What are you a doctor of,' I asked?

'I'm Doctor Doc', he said with pride opening his arms wide.

'That's a new one on me. What do you do?' I asked.

'I doctor documents', he said.

I must have had a baffled look on my face as he continued. 'It all starts when someone steals a document, say a Giro,' he said.

'That's a cheque you get when you're unemployed with your benefit that you can cash at a Post Office,' I said.

'That's right but it's not a normal cheque that you put in the bank and wait three days for your money. You get the cash instantly that's why it has better security than a cheque. With a normal cheque the banks have three days to find out if you have tampered with it; the Post Office counter staff has only a few seconds.

As I said someone steals a giro and it gets passed to me,' he said patiently. 'I then change the payee's name to match a stolen driving licence I have and pass it back. The person who stole it cashes it and walks off with the money and I take a percentage. It's as simple as that'.

'You must be very good; the backgrounds are printed with lots of wavy lines that react to solvents and water when you try to change the characters', I said.

'Yes, it takes a lot of time an effort. I must use tiny amounts of solvent to dissolve the name as they print it on a dot matrix printer. That's a computer printer that uses an ink ribbon like a typewriter. If I use too much solvent, I dissolve the background, and the post office would spot the alteration.

I was making a good living until the Professor caught me. Now I work for him and make an even better one and I'm no longer a criminal.'

'What do you do for him,' I asked?

'I understand your going to be the Professor's son-in-law so I suppose I can tell you'. 'He has an arrangement with a couple of security printers down South and when they come up with a new design they send him samples, he brings them to me, and I see if I can break them. Sometimes I can break it easily and I make suggestions on what they can do. They get to see the evidence bags of documents that have been altered from current trials as they need to give expert witness statements. That way they learn what is being done so they can change the design so it can't be done again.

He gave me a choice, work for him or be deported again. I had already been deported twice so the court would give me a long stretch before deporting me again for a third offence.'

'Deported, again?'

'I was sent over here originally twenty years ago but I didn't last very long as the government had just changed the pension book design, and I was caught. I was very stupid as I tried to cash the book myself saying I was collecting my ill father's pension. The design was out of date and the post office called the police. I got a year for that first time and deported to Nigeria. So, I went back to 'The School' and told them how I got caught.'

'The school?'

'We have a school for fraud in Nigeria. Anyone who gets deported goes back so the next ones sent over don't make the same mistakes.'

'It sounds highly organised.'

'It is, then after a year I was given a new passport and a new name and back I came; I lasted five years that time, got two years in jail and deported. The police told me not to come back again otherwise they would throw away the key next time. The third time I came back I lasted seven years. They nicknamed me Dr Doc because that's what I did but they never found me. Then the Professor caught me and gave me the chance to change my life from being hunted to being safe.

So, what's your problem?'

'I explained about the paper, and I need to reproduce a watermark,' I said. 'Normally it's created when the paper is made; we have to create it on the press.'

'In short what you need is a paper that looks like a security paper without all the bells and whistles,' he said.

'That's right. But I can't find one.'

'You could use recycled paper it has the weight and feel and looks a bit grey as it still has the ink residue but it's not UV dull as the manufacturers use chlorine bleach to get rid of the ink and that causes fluorescing'.

'I never thought of using recycled as I don't believe in it'.

'You don't believe in recycling; don't you want to save the planet?' he asked.

'Not by recycling paper; yes, we need to recycle anything where the resource is finite. Paper is a renewable. I think it is better to burn it for energy rather than contaminate the planet with the horrendous chemicals like the chlorine you mentioned they must use to get the paper anywhere near white again. I believe in Power and Light companies.'

'I've never heard of Power and Light companies; what are they?' he asked.

'It's all to do with the waste in your dustbin, what the Americans call garbage. It's collected from your house, and they tip it into a hole in the ground. Now they are running out of waste tips, so they are building hills or dumping it in the sea. Staten Island off New York is the largest manmade structure on earth at its peak 13,000 tons of rubbish was added every day. That garbage is slowly decomposing giving off methane gas, which is one of the worst greenhouse gases. It is a legacy we are leaving our children and grandchildren for years to come.

Instead, I believe we should take that rubbish and burn it instead. That combination of packaging and general waste needs to be burnt so the energy contained can be released and put to good use. We must think of it as 'Green' energy.

With a Power and Light system, you build an incinerator near to say a hospital maybe half a mile away. You deliver the waste from the community then burn it capturing the CO_2 as a liquid, not releasing it into the atmosphere. Then use the heat to generate electricity to power the hospital and keep it warm. At night the energy is used to chill water to run the hospital's air conditioning system the next day. What is left is just ash taking up a fraction of the landfill that would have been needed, and it's inert not damaging the environment. You then sell any spare electricity to the National Grid.

The CO_2 could be stored in old coal mines in barrels made from recycled plastics; putting it back underground where it came from.

It's better to burn paper; then use virgin paper rather than recycled, as paper maker's plant three young trees when they cut down one; young trees absorb more CO_2 than older trees; when they get old, they give off CO_2. All this reduces the cost of running the hospital while solving a major environment problem.

I think that anything where they use chipped-up wood such as flat-pack furniture they should use recycled plastic and use the wood for green energy instead. If they made kitchen units out of solid recycled plastic it would never rot and all you would have to do is buy new doors and you have a new kitchen. Now you must rip out the entire kitchen and chuck it in a waste tip; then replace the whole thing again in a few years.'

'Put like that it seems so obvious; why doesn't the government encourage it?'

I don't know; I think there may be some Power & Light units in the States, but I don't know of any over here.'

'If you go and try the recycled paper, I'll do some tests about creating watermarks. I'll give you a call if I have any luck.'

At last recycled paper finally had a useful role, well in my mind anyway. I bought some reams of recycled paper from the merchants and Brian tried it. It certainly looked the part; it was a bit grey from the ink residue and felt like the real thing when you rubbed it between the fingers, if a bit thicker. It would all depend on what the fake watermark looked like.

The Doctor phoned about two weeks later.

'I have done the watermark trials with about thirty different substances from baby oil to engine grease,' he said. 'It's been a matter of finding something that will flow on a printing press without evaporating but then penetrate the paper just enough to make it translucent; most just soaked in making the paper look like last night's fish and chip paper.

There is one that seems to do the job, but you will have to do a full trial on the press to be sure. It's a form of petroleum jelly a bit like Vaseline but rather obscure, it's normally used on army tank shells. Try it and if it doesn't work, I'll look at some more.

If it works, I can order a larger amount through a third party, so it won't be traced back to you.'

Chapter 11

Once again, I met the Professor at his boat's mooring but this time there was an extra excitement in the air, a feeling of expectation of things about to happen. The Professor was bouncing around the main cabin, arranging the table and chairs.

'Ten years ago, when I started this group they hated my guts', he said. 'They thought I had forced them to agree to the proposal but after some hectic years, matters settled down and now we have mutual respect, and they see the benefits. I certainly couldn't have put such a proposal to them at the beginning.'

The sound of a car pulling up in the boat yard caused us to pause looking at each other.

'This is the day,' he said, 'it all comes down to you Joe.'

Nothing like adding to the pressure, I thought.

It was "Manchester". His bodyguard come chauffeur came round the car opening the rear door so his passenger could get out.

'Professor, Joe,' greeted "Manchester".

'"Manchester",' the Professor replied.

Turning "Manchester" said to his driver, 'Go and park some place. I'll phone you when I need you.'

Two more cars came in the yard dropping off the passengers, each being greeted in a similar way.

'We'll pick the others up further down the Mere,' said the Professor.

Two more stops and the nine most powerful criminal leaders in the country were assembled. Each one looked like an ordinary businessman but with an added air of menace; one made me sweat just looking at him. He hadn't said a word not greeting any of the others just stared at "Manchester" with a look so cold it was icy.

'Now we are moored away from eavesdroppers please take your seats,' said the Professor.

'At the end is Joe whose idea you have come to hear.'

Ten faces turned towards me, and I knew real fear for the first time in my life. The adrenaline was flowing through my body causing my stomach to cramp and my nerves tingle; I felt like I was about to be sick. I had done high power presentations before but nothing like this and not to this sort of audience; my legs felt so weak I thought I would fall over when I stood. To my right was a flip chart I had prepared, it was looking a bit worn where I had practised. First to myself then time and again to a video camera until I had it word perfect.

After the first faltering words I got into my stride going through everything just as I had done with "Manchester" finally handing out the samples. The Professor explained they needn't worry about fingerprints as everything would be shredded in the cabin before being incinerated.

"Birmingham" shuffled through the samples then stopped, looked at me saying, 'I don't see any for M&S.'

'We can't achieve anything that wouldn't be spotted immediately. As you now M&S is the best protected; it's almost banknote quality,' I answered.

'I can't emphasise enough that secrecy is the key. If they have as much as a hint of what is about to happen, they will spot everyone. It needs to be kept just to your most trusted people.'

'We need to talk about this,' said "Manchester" to the group.

'Joe, can you leave us,' said the Professor. 'I'll call you when we're ready.'

'Who is this guy,' said "London"? 'Can we trust him?'

'I've had him checked and he is exactly who he says he is,' said the Professor.

'Yes, but Eton and Oxford. I know what you have done "Professor", but he's got to be a plant but it's so obvious and to what end? I can't see what the Old Bill would gain.'

'They know who we are or are they trying to trap us, trying to catch us with our hands in the till?' added Cardiff.

The discussion went on for some time until "Liverpool" summed it up. 'I vote we go along with him but at the first sign of a double-cross we top him and take over the operation.'

In truth I was glad to get out of there, the air on deck smelt so fresh after that cabin. I just sat staring across the Mere at some sailing dinghies racing round a course marked with buoys, the wild screams of the children mixing with the slap of the wavelets against the boat. The adrenaline slowly abated until I was just sitting staring at the water. I needed a drink; I had never craved alcohol especially at 10 in the morning then I remembered the "Professor" kept some cigars in the cockpit for visitors. I hadn't smoked for years but I needed something to calm my nerves. The smoke caught the back of my throat making me cough, my eyes seemed to bulge, and I was so dizzy I nearly fell in. Then the nicotine hit my bloodstream, and my body relaxed. I threw it away only half smoked vowing not to smoke again but I felt better, more resigned to whatever awaited me.

It was nearly an hour before the cabin door opened, and the "Professor" called me in gesturing to my seat. "Liverpool" seemed to have been elected spokesman as he said, 'Joe you have achieved something no one else has ever managed. We will all cooperate and have agreed to your proposal but with one condition. £75 million is not enough to make it worthwhile as a one-shot scam so we're making it £750 million and each one of us will give you £100,000 buy in. We are also reducing your take and the "Professor's" to 5%. That will still give you £37 million each, tops.'

I didn't know what to say I just stood there dumb struck with the enormity of what they were saying.

'Excuse us,' said the "Professor", 'I need to talk to Joe up top.'

'They're crazy; it's bound to fail; it will leak out. £750 million that's 15 million vouchers at £50 each. It can't be done that's just too many we haven't got the capacity to print that many and where is the paper coming from; the police will arrest all the front-line people, and we'll get caught; we'll go to prison?'

'It was something you said that gave them the idea,' said the Professor.

'Me? What did I say?'

'That anyone getting caught passing vouchers would only get a slap on the wrist.'

'That's right but with that many they will all get caught. Then the next ones in the chain and so on back to us.'

'The bosses are quite happy with the pushers getting caught if they get the spoils. You don't know the law of the jungle. Anyone fingering someone else would not live to regret it.'

'What about the production?'

'You were only planning on printing for eight hours a night we'll make it fourteen hours a night. They can take over as soon as the day shift finishes at six and be away by eight the next morning and we have six more shops opening. It's still Boxing Day 1981 giving you 12 months and they're calling it 'B' day, that's a code name for secrecy not a sick joke.'

'And the paper?'

'Now you have identified the type we need we can just buy it in bulk quite openly from the trade. We'll set up a paper importing company and bring it in legitimately then when it's all over the company will simple evaporate along with all its paperwork so nothing can be traced.

We better go back and tell them what you have decided.'

Sitting back in my seat I said. 'OK but are you sure your people can keep it secret?'

'Yes,' said "Liverpool" 'how about at the printing stage?'

'I've just talked it through with the "Professor". By stepping up production to 14 hrs a night and the extra units coming on stream I think we can do it. Can you handle breaking the bulk down into small lots and the distribution?'

'Yes,' said "Liverpool", 'we've discussed that. It will be taken care of.'

'Are we all agreed,' asked 'Liverpool', '£750 million Boxing Day 1981?'

They all raised their hands.

'If you let us down,' "London" said in a quiet menacing voice, 'you will be lucky to spend the rest of your life in a wheelchair.'

Chapter 12

It began. The most hectic year of my life even though I wasn't directly involved with production of the vouchers they seemed to call me with any little hitch. I also had a full-time job as MD of the ConPrint franchise.

The paper importing company was set up with directors of impeccable backgrounds, all totally fictitious. Two units on an industrial estate near the M1/M25 acted as warehousing with another duplicate set up at the other end of the M1 near Leeds. They were ideally situated to receive bulk paper from the importers in one unit and printed stock each morning from the franchisees.

Other ex-prisoners became delivery drivers picking up the previous night's production from each franchise and delivering it to the print warehouses, where they were repacked it into smaller parcels for distribution to the eight gangs.

Ironically, we found a paper maker in India who made recycled paper from waste sent from the UK in empty shipping containers. The UK was quite happy meeting its recycling quotas by dumping its waste on another country and the Indian state with the paper mill making 'environmentally friendly paper' where totally unconcerned about the chlorine and other waste chemicals it dumped in the sea. The large orders we placed meant they were making money, so everyone was happy, except perhaps the fish.

Brian trained the new guys coming out of prison. He was the perfect face for them to know. If he said, 'Do it this way and keep your mouth shut,' that is exactly what they did. Each franchise printed just one type of store voucher so there was only one set of printing plates to keep secure.

I only saw Amanda about once a month during that year. She was either away doing something for the Professor or I was at the other end of the country. We would meet at some hotel or other usually both tired from driving and over-work. We became comfortable in each other's company; a quiet meal somewhere and a night of gentle lovemaking. There was never that sense of occasion we had at the Midland. How I dreamed of St Kitts and making love to Amanda every day.

The five girls, all in their late teens or early twenties; looked like they were going on a picnic with their summer clothes and baskets on that lovely day in May. They looked out of place when they turned into the road leading under Manchester's Piccadilly station. Down there were numerous businesses under the arches of the old Victorian station where car repairers had lockups and delivery firms had storage or a distribution hub. It was busy with traffic going in and out all day; a dark and forbidding place with a river running through the middle like some Machiavellian underworld.

The girls threaded their way through the traffic until they came to one of the more decrepit looking lockups, which they entered through a small door at the side of a pair of large wooden double ones. Anyone seeing them would think it odd but knew it would not be healthy to ask any questions as the lockup belonged to "Manchester".

Inside there was enough space for a van to enter and back up to a raised concrete loading platform. Where more closed doors at the back of the platform meant no one could see into the lockup when the outer doors were opened.

The girls went through the inner door turning on the lights as they went. It was like a large cavern with three rows of long tables each being stacked with paper and lit by overhead fluorescent lights hung from chains from the domed arched roof. Just then a low rumble started overhead growing in volume as the InterCity train left for London. The girls placed their baskets on a table in the far corner next to an electric kettle and a sink full of dirty coffee mugs before going to the tables. Three went to the back row and two to the front with each table being sectioned off from its neighbour in the row by large vertical dividers. On each divider three different cards were mounted with vouchers. Each one reflected the colourful piles of cards and vouchers stacked on the tables. They were there to remind the girls how the different stores inserted their vouchers in the gift cards. Some were stuck in with a stub to the voucher while others were wire stapled. Some were just inserted loose into a pocket inside the card.

The girls set too with a practiced ease picking a couple of vouchers from the various piles then picking up a greetings card, quickly fixing them together. Each one was put in a small box that had the name of the store, then stacked them on a pallet. The chatted as they worked mostly about boys or a new dress they wanted. All except a quiet black girl at the front who worked in silence not being part of the group behind who were all daughters of "Manchester's" subordinates. Rosie was in charge and Hump's girlfriend, "Manchester's" son and 1st lieutenant. Humphrey was his name, but no one dare call him that to his face except his mother; everyone else called him Hump after his liking for the ladies.

It was Rosie who got up when a bell rang from someone at the door. Looking through the spyhole Rosie recognised Bert, one of the regular drivers, who waved and went back to his van when Rosie knocked twice on the door. Rosie opened the big double doors and Bert backed up to the loading ramp so Rosie could close the outer doors again.

'Hi Rosie,' he said, 'I've another delivery for you; that makes the third this week. What's in them? I know, you can't tell me otherwise you would have to shoot me.'

Rosie laughed as she took the parcels from him, stacking them on a trolley.

'You're right there,' she said.

As soon as he left, she locked the outer doors then opened the inner ones pulling the trolley behind her.

'How many more of these are there,' called one of the girls named Maggie.

'I don't know,' replied Rosie, 'I think this is just the beginning.'

'That's good I want to earn lots for Alton Towers,' said Maggie.

The endless stream of vouchers continued as the number of different stores increased until the cavern was stacked to the roof with pallets of boxes.

The girls completed their task. It was September 1981, and they were on a high. Not only had they finished well inside the deadline set by "Manchester" but they had money in their pockets. Earlier in the year they had gone to Alton Towers. Now they were going to Blackpool for their weekend away for thrilling rides and flirting with the boys. But this time they would go without Rosie; her flirting days were over as she had just become engaged to Hump.

'I don't mind,' she told them. 'I've still got to do the schedules for 'B' day, and I need the peace and quiet without you lot chattering in my ear. Anyway, Hump is looking after me over the weekend and has promised to take me to 'Sandals' in the Bahamas when this is over.'

'Ooh,' the girls said as they went out laughing.

Chapter 13

DD was not born a psychopath he was the sum of all the people he had met and the events in his life. Everyone called him DD even the teachers, but they thought it was because of his name, Derek Davidson but he was called DD by the girls, and it meant Deadly Dull in a nasty cruel put down. It wasn't because he wasn't intelligent; he was always in the top quarter of any exam results. It was because nobody really noticed him. He was always the last to be picked for any team, football, cricket, there was always that phrase from one of the team captains, 'Oh DD can be on my team'. The girls ignored him; they always went for the good-looking ones; even when there were more girls than boys DD sat in the corner alone.

His parents' house never had the luxury of a bathroom just a tin bath hanging on a nail outside. Every Friday his father would take it down, putting it in front of the gas fire in the kitchen; then filling it by connecting a hose pipe to the spout on the gas Ascot water heater over the kitchen sink. The water made a crashing sound as it bounced on the bottom of the tin bath; the steam rising, filling the room with its warm embrace. It was the only time DD felt truly loved as his father scrubbed him from top to toe, making sure DD cleaned behind his ears as he said, 'You must always keep yourself clean and fresh for the ladies. You wouldn't want to put them off by being smelly; adding you really are your father's son.'

His mother was a tart wanting to go to the pub every night where she flirted with the men in the bar while his father watched from the shadows; resulting in loud arguments every time they came home. DD's father was like him; quiet, rather plain and hardworking, he wanted an old-fashioned wife, who would bake, wash his clothes and be content to stay at home and in his bed. He didn't blame his wife; the only time they had had sex was on their wedding night when Derek was conceived, after that she refused saying he was a freak and didn't want sex with him again. In the end, he just couldn't cope anymore; he went to get some cigarettes one day from the corner shop and didn't come back. DD was only seven; he had lost the only person who loved him.

He might have turned out as a clone of his father if he had met a homespun girl like the one his father wanted, he would have been content, hurting no one, a drone, a worker in society but his mother didn't love him, he was just there in the background fending for himself. Then she made that step from tart to prostitute. The men from the pub now came home with her each night going upstairs while he sat in the kitchen reading his comic, the Dandy. He could hear their laughter from upstairs, the noise of the bed springs; then a knock, knock, knocking as the headboard banged against the wall.

He went into himself, fantasising about the characters in his comic, and the day his father would come back and love him, but he never did. He longed to be the character from his comic, Desperate Dan and not just DD. Eating Cow Pie charging upstairs throwing those men out and climbing into bed with his mother, being held in her loving arms, protecting her.

He grew up unwanted, unloved in that lonely house, rejected by the people he loved, he cried out to be wanted, to be loved.

At eleven the comic changed to the Eagle and DD became Dan Dare. He longed to fly amongst the stars with his new hero, fighting baddies and saving the World. His mother got old before her time and the men rougher now coming from the street corner near the docks. Sometimes he heard his mother scream, appearing with a black eye and once a broken arm. His mother screamed for the last time when he was thirteen. It was a long time after the front door banged shut that he ventured upstairs.

There was an evil smell of despair in that room; unwashed bodies, dirty bed clothes, clothing scattered across the floor where they had been discarded and his half naked mother lying on the bed, her head at an unnatural angle, eyes staring, still looking for something but never finding it.

The orphanage tried to make DD happy, but they could not get past the shell he had around him. He grew up in his fantasy world where he was handsome, adored by everyone, the team captain; he dreamt of having a relationship, a loving wife and children to love; it just wasn't going to happen.

Social Services found him a job in an old-fashioned back street printer as a Compositor, a typesetter; he stood at a bench all day gathering letters that had been cast from molten lead, into a 'composing stick'; the capital letters from the Upper Case and the smaller ones from the Lower Case. Line after line of other people's words, other people's lives. The shop was old, probably pre 1st World War; dark and dirty, the cases of type full of dust that got up his nose.

At night he would go to his dingy one-room bedsit on the top floor of a Victorian four-story house. In the summer it was hot when the sun streamed through the dormer window and in the winter, ice formed on the inside of the glass. The bathroom was one floor down, the landlady kept it clean, but it was never heated and the water often only just warm. It didn't worry DD, but he missed the heat.

Each Friday he would have Fish and Chips on the way home from work before the ritual of the Friday night bath. Other days he would warm the Mutton Stew he had made on the Sunday, on the gas ring in the hearth that was his only means of cooking; each day adding a few more vegetables to make it last longer.

But on Saturdays he would go to Sandown, Kempton Park, Epsom or Ascot, wherever there was a horse race meeting. On the excursion bus from London there was a feeling of camaraderie as everyone was going to the same place for the same reason, to enjoy the day. The beer flowed and the songs sang, mixed in with the rough banter of the East End, DD felt part of it.

It was when they all got off that DD felt lonely. There was the heaving crowd of humanity in Tattersall's that ebbed and flowed from the parade ring to the bookies and back. He was like a rock in the middle that everyone flowed around but did not notice. DD liked to stand by the rail, near the finishing post, feeling the ground shake as the horses and riders galloped by, imagining himself on the back of the leading horse, champion jockey, then to the Winner's Enclosure and the presentation of the trophy to the adoration of the crowd.

It was rather masochistic for DD to go racing but he wanted to belong, and the noise and colour of racing was so opposite to what he was; it attracted him at the same time as it revolted him. He hated the couples and the families having a day out enjoying themselves while he felt sick to his stomach; but most of all he hated the women at Ascot on Ladies Day. He would watch them parading through the crowd in front of the men like a herd of prize cows with their udders on show

He never bet; it just wasn't in his nature. To take a risk was inviting disaster, he knew he would lose. To contact another human being was to invite rejection, so he didn't. He just kept all the emotion, the dreams, the need, the desire, inside himself; festering into a hard core that made him hate the world and everyone in it.

Then one Friday his world changed.

'Don't come back on Monday,' he was told, he was redundant. Replaced by some young girl with an IBM Golf Ball typewriter and a mini skirt, the lead type melted down for scrap. The years of tradition and loyalty thrown aside, like yesterday's fish and chip papers, and him with it.

Saturday was Sandown Park, and his life changed again when Derek the Dip was born. This time the crowds worked in his favour. The press of humanity in Tattersall's allowed him to relieve today's winner of having to carry the heavy load of cash or another's wallet. This time those long fingers, trained for years to pick up the smallest of lead type, could remove the wings from a butterfly while it was still flying without the butterfly knowing. Then blend in with the crowd as if invisible. It was this innate skill that brought him to the attention of "London".

No one worked the racing crowds of the London courses without his approval and contributing to his coffers. But "London" did not have to persuade DD to join his ranks for DD at last found a place where he was wanted. He was a natural, working the crowds passing on each new lift to his runner, a young boy who would disappear stashing it away somewhere safe then coming back for the next one. But it wasn't necessary, nobody challenged DD for they never saw him, in the end he dispensed with the boy and put the lifts in secret pockets in his long coat.

He was also a valued asset when information was wanted about another gang's territory or operation. DD's natural invisibility meant he could roam at will another gang's patch without their knowledge. It was this ability that brought him to Manchester.

"London" wanted to expand his Casino and Strip Joint Empire and set his sights on Birmingham and Manchester. Birmingham was geographically closer but there was something appealing about bearding his old enemy "Manchester" on his own patch. He sent DD to poke around in "Manchester's" operation. It was nearly lunch time on the third day when DD was following Hump. A man in his late 20s five foot seven or eight, slim athletic build, dark wavy hair and dark features.

His clothes were like a uniform dark leather jacket, jeans and winkle picker shoes that turned up like Ali Baba's; the small rucksack over one shoulder the only thing out of place.

DD had followed him from their backstreet office to a non-descript lockup in the railway arches under Piccadilly Station. Making sure he wasn't observed Hump went to a small door at the side of the main one and knocked with an obviously pre-arranged signal. About a minute later the door opened and one of the most beautiful young black girls DD had ever seen literally flung herself at him. Kissing him so hard and long one would have thought she hadn't seen him for months. Pushing her slowly off, the man looked around and not observing anyone looking at them stepped inside and closed the door.

An hour later the door opened, and the man stepped out only to be pulled half back in again as the girl entwined herself around him, doing everything she could to entice him back in the warehouse. Eventually he pushed her away and closed the door.

Turning and walking away his smile said it all; and DD had a very sick feeling at the pit of stomach. DD stayed there all day but no one else entered or left until about six when the man returned and after his knock the girl emerged wearing a printed raincoat covered in bright flowers. The man locked the door, and they walked off hand in hand her head only coming up to his shoulder despite her high heeled shoes.

DD was booked into a cheap B&B, laying on his bed seeing that beautiful girl in his mind and imagining what those young lovers had been doing in the warehouse. Slowly that sick feeling became a hard lump in his stomach. He couldn't sleep, his imagination running wild. The lump began to burn and slowly it turned to hatred about his lonely life, without love, without physical contact, without sex his need for release overpowering.

He got up to do the one thing he said he wouldn't; use a prostitute. During his wonderings around Manchester, he saw where the prostitutes worked, and the punters crawled by in their cars to assess what was on offer and ask the price. There was one street in particular that would suit his purpose; it was at the side of a park where the railings had gaps into which the girls would fade when a police car came past.

Lena told me her story when I was investigating the fraud. It was not directly part of it, but I'm including it as it shows one of the ways an innocent can be trapped into the criminal world. A criminal does not care about people, just seeing them as something to be used and exploited.

Roy Adams

Lena's parents came from Poland in the '40s escaping from Hitler's tyranny only to be killed in a freak car accident when Lena was two years old. In the next fourteen years Lena lived in three care homes and two foster homes. She was always petite which made her look younger than what she was resulting in the foster parents treating like a child. On her sixteenth birthday she just walked out heading for London to the streets that were not paved with gold. A bed at the YWCA and a job at McDonalds was her first step to adulthood but a manager with roaming hands and a quick temper meant that she was out of work without a reference.

Then her knight in shining armour came along. Leck was also Polish; down from Manchester visiting relations in the local Polish community. Leck took her to meet his uncle and their family. The food, the music, the very sound of the language seemed natural to her even though she could not understand a word. They visited the Polish Centre where the sights and sounds seemed to tug at her very soul; she thought she had found her roots.

Then Leck came to the end of his visit and had to go back to Manchester. The thought of being alone once again in London filled her with dread; so much so that when he asked her if she wanted to go with him, she jumped at the chance.

The first month with him was like a dream come true. They were together in his expensive flat most of the day where they made love often. Each evening, he had to go out for a short time to take care of his business interests. When she asked what they were she was told not to worry about such things but be ready for him when he returned.

It was Leck who introduced her to heroin subtly at first.

'To enhance their lovemaking,' he said.

Then it became more frequent; then each day she had to have her fix. Until the day he wouldn't give her anymore unless she earned it. It was then Lena became a prostitute. That was nearly twenty years ago. She hadn't done badly, managing to steer clear of the perverts and major diseases. She had a little in the bank even though Leck still took the lions share.

Lena didn't see him coming, one second, he wasn't there and then he was. She jumped when the voice behind her asked, 'How much?'

He had thought she was about 20 but now he was closer he realised she wouldn't see 30 again. The heavy makeup and what had to be a wig went well with her tight t-shirt and mini skirt or was it a wide belt. Her legs seemed to be so long with their sky-high heeled shoes they were out of proportion to her body. It was then he realised she was rather petit; maybe he had picked the wrong one.

'Where's your car?' the girl asked.

'Haven't got one', said DD, 'we'll go in the park'.

'50 quid.........in advance'.

DD produced the money which disappeared into her gold-coloured bag hanging on a chain from her shoulder.

'Come on then', she said, turning to walk through the gap in the railings behind her, swinging her bum in a way she thought was provocative but looked more like she was about to fall off those sky-high heels.

Taking his hand, she led him down a tarmacked path deeper into the gardens. 'There's a quiet spot over here on the grass where I can lay a nice blanket, and we won't be disturbed.'

Over her shoulder she asked, 'Have you got a condom?'

'No, I thought not', and walked over to a holdall she had hidden in the bushes. Bending over she rummaged in the bag while wiggling her hips the short skirt rose showing DD exactly what he was buying.

Kneeling she hitched her skirt all the way up saying, 'Come a little closer it's so dark in here I can't see you; I need to slip on the condom.'

Opening his coat, she felt inside for his fly. You needn't have brought a police truncheon to hit me over the head; I'll come quietly, well not too quietly', she laughed.

'That's not a truncheon. That's my cock'.

'Jesus Christ', she exclaimed. 'I can't take that; it's fucking huge. I don't mind big men but that......that belongs in a zoo. You're a fucking freak; here I'll give you your money back', as she scrambled in her bag, throwing the money at him.

'No', he shouted. 'I've paid for it, now I'm going to have it', as her lunged for here but she was too quick; ducking under his arm she ran as if her life was in danger. First there was no sound then the clicking of her heels as she found the path and as DD watched, the moon came out revealing her white bottom as it bobbed back in forth like a fleeing doe, her skirt still up above her waist.

DD followed, reaching the road she had disappeared. Following the railings he approached the other girls but as he did, they shrank back into the shadows of the park; the word had gone out; no one wanted him.

The rage of his manhood's rejection was still there in the morning as he stood watching the warehouse. It got hotter and fiercer as he saw the couple arrive; the young man fondled her, his hands on her breasts as she unlocked the door. Turning in his arms she pulled him by the waist into the warehouse and the door slammed shut.

DD waited for the man to reappear; it seemed like an eternity, DD's imagination working him into a frenzy. Finally, the door opened the man emerged. DD waited two agonising minutes until he was sure the man wasn't coming back then walked over to the door and gave the signal he had heard, three quick taps a pause then two more. The door opened quickly, and the girl's smiling face appeared.

'You came back', she started to say, only to see a grey middle-aged man standing there and she didn't understand, then everything went black.

DD saw that smiling welcoming face that he knew was not for him all he could see was a red mist and he punched her straight between the eyes, knocking her back onto the floor. Kicking the door shut behind him he tore at his clothes then bending over ripped the clothes from her body, ravaging her savagely tearing into her body, rupturing her internally.

This was not sex, not even lust, there was no gratification, this was revenge, revenge for all the hurt in his life, the loneliness, the longing and his hatred of all women.

Hump was nearly halfway back when he remembered his wallet; it had fallen out of his jacket in the warehouse; he had meant to pick it up but was rather distracted. His first thought was to leave it until lunchtime, but he needed his driving licence to hire a car that morning. Returning he couldn't understand why the door was not quite closed, he was sure he had shut it securely on the way out. Swinging the door open it took a few seconds for him to understand what was happening but then grabbed a wooden chair, swung it high and crashed it down on the back of DD's head knocking him to one side. Then he saw poor Rosie, the girl he gave up all others for, the girl he was planning on spending his life with. Her naked broken body laid on that cold floor, her face broken and blood all over her lower body. The rage swelled up in him as he brought the chair down on DD's head again and again until his scalp was hanging off exposing the skull beneath.

Hump picked up the phone from the workbench. 'Dad', he said, 'Rosie's been raped. No, I've done for him. Send an ambulance quick and a doctor she's going to need both'.

Hump knelt on the floor; where he tenderly gathered Rosie in his arms and cried for her.

It seemed like a lifetime for help to arrive. A living nightmare as Rosie moaned with pain in her unconscious state as Hump cradled her to him, making soothing sounds to calm her. Finally, his father arrived drawing Hump aside to let the doctor at Rosie.

'Who is he', "Manchester" asked as he pointed to DD's slumped body.

'I don't now', said Hump as he rolled DD onto his back.

'Poor Rosie', he cried.

Hump searched DD's pockets until he found a wallet. 'His name is Derek Davidson and he's from London', he said.

'That's Derek the Dip', said "Manchester". 'He's part of "London's" mob. He must have been up here scouting'. It was then they heard DD moan.

'He's not dead, said "M".

'He soon will be', said Hump.

'No', commanded "Manchester", 'we'll use him to send a message to "London" and any other gangs who want to move in on us that it's a no-go area'.

'Contact the Professor; tell him I need an urgent meeting as there is something he needs to arrange otherwise it will be a full war with "London"'.

Chapter 14

Sitting round the kitchen table drinking tea was usually a happy friendly time; Ju made China tea for herself but Assam for Amanda, the Professor and me; but this day was different. Ju had had a letter from Li; her husband had died after being kicked in the head by a horse.

'Ju, what's her life going to be like,' asked the Professor?

'Not good,' said Ju, 'with no children her whole life was around her husband and horse racing. She will be at a total loss.'

'You're her only relative. Do you think she would like to come and live with us?'

'She has often spoken about our life here in England. I think she would like that.'

'Then phone her, we have plenty of space here with Agnes gone and Amanda soon to move out.'

At that point the phone rang at the Professor's elbow with that strident shrill demand 'talk to me, talk to me' sound interrupting the conversation. He picked up the handset and just listened. As he did so his face got redder and redder until he slowly put the phone down staring at it as if it was something malignant saying with a single uncharacteristic explosive word, 'Shit'.

Turning to Ju and Amanda he said, 'I apologise my dears for my language. Joe, I need to talk to you come to my study'.

Sitting at his desk he was obviously agitated filling his pipe so hard with tobacco it wouldn't suck so had to take it out again. At last, he got it going and with his head in a cloud of smoke turned to me.

'One of "London's" gang has been on a scouting visit to Manchester and found the voucher warehouse,' he said.

'Did he steal anything,' I asked?

'Much worse "Manchester's" future daughter-in-law was working there on her own and he raped her. The Manchester gangs have united and are threatening a mass visit to "London". This is the end of 'B' day, unless we can come up with an answer'.

A meeting aboard the boat was scheduled for three days later. This time the atmosphere was not amicable, and "Manchester" did not come alone. Hump was with him and a 'new face' that was to be known as "Moss Side".

Moss Side was an area of Manchester with a predominance of people from the Caribbean. The gangs were very local to an area or even street, controlling the drugs and prostitution. Gang fights and knifings were a daily occurrence and drive by shootings not uncommon. There had never been one gang strong enough to control the rest or one voice of reason; until now. The attack on Rosie was seen as an attack on one of their own and a single voice drew them together into one cohesive group. The voice said, 'Join with "Manchester" against "London" and they did.'

It was "London's" turn to be picked up last and the atmosphere was hostile. "London" sat in his normal chair and not a word was spoken as we left the mooring, cruising to an isolated spot and anchored. The "Professor" came down and took the chairman's seat.

'I will not bother with introductions,' he said, 'as we all know why we are here but just welcome 'Moss Side' to this group as a new full member and Hump, "Manchester's" son for this one meeting.

To keep tempers under control and to stop this meeting degenerating you will all address anything you say through me 'The Chair' and for brevity you will refer to each other by your initials as usual. "Manchester" requested this meeting so he will open.'

'Three days ago, one of "L's" men raped my future daughter-in-law. She is still in hospital and there is still some uncertainty if she will ever be able to have children. My son Hump will execute him, and the usual message will be sent to all the members of this group.'

'I apologise to "M" for my man overstepping the boundary and to Hump for his loss, but I will deal with him myself. Give him back to me and we will end the matter.'

'No,' exploded Hump, 'I will kill him.'

'If one of "M's" people executes "DD" then we will come in force to Manchester and see who comes out top dog.'

'Sit down Hump,' said "M". 'We have an impasse, Mr Chair.'

'Are you both agreed that "DD" is to be executed for his crime, and neither will accept the other carrying out the sentence?'

They both nodded slowly and deliberately.

'Then will you both agree that the sentence can be carried out by a third party not attached to either of you?'

Again, they both nodded.

'Then I suggest we use the services of 'The Shadow''.

'No,' said "L", 'Joe will execute him.'

'Me, execute him', I spluttered.

'We will have a recess. I need to talk to Joe,' said the Professor.

'Joe; go topside. I'll join you in a minute.'

'What's the idea,' asked the Professor.

'You know I've never trusted him,' said "L". 'Call it a test. If he's legit he'll go through with it but if he's a plant and refuses. You know what happens then.'

'Me? I can't even kill a spider.'

'Yes. Execute him, kill him. This is a cruel world you have entered with basic rules, nothing else will do. If it's not done quickly there will be an all-out war and 'B' day won't happen.

It can't be done by one of "L's" gang because no one will believe him and if someone from "M's" gang does it, you will have a war. If you don't the whole thing is over and a lot of innocent bystanders will get hurt, maybe killed from the fallout.

You must show decisive leadership. They know this is your show, so you must command their respect by taking action. Don't forget L's warning about the wheelchair; if you don't do this you can forget the wheelchair he will demand your head.

One good thing to come out of this is the Moss Side gangs weren't cooperating, but this has brought them together, as one.

The Shadow can help you, but you must do it, and they all must know it has been done.'

We went into utter silence and took our seats as everyone looked at me.

Swallowing I said, 'I'll carry out the execution.'

'As "M" stated the usual message will be sent to each one of you,' said the Professor.

'I want the part that violated Rosie to feed to my fish', added Hump.

After a short pause "L" and "M" nodded their agreement.

'Perhaps we can gain something out of this unfortunate incident,' said the Professor. 'Have you heard of the Soviet printing works in Africa?'

All the faces at the table looked blank so he went on.

'At the height of the cold war the Soviets set up a currency printing works in one of their African satellites with the idea of devaluing Western currency by flooding the world with counterfeits. They printed billions of US dollars, but they ended up in vaults all over the Third World but very few ended up in the USA. The Americans know all about it, which is why they have never changed the design, it would bankrupt too many of those Third World countries causing Worldwide panic. The Americans go to great lengths to make sure they don't turn up in the USA.

The Africans also printed billions of British notes but unlike the dollars, which were near perfect they made a mistake on them and were never circulated. The Soviets instructed that they were to be destroyed but no one is sure they were. The British government has been in fear of them being used for years. I don't know how he got hold of them, but the Doctor brought some back with him after his last trip to Nigeria.'

'Hand these around but keep them in the plastic pockets to keep them free of fingerprints.'

'They look good to me,' said "Birmingham".

'Look at the watermark.'

'So? It's the Queens head.'

'It's facing the wrong way. It should be facing to the right into the banknote, not to the left.'

'That's all very interesting,' said 'Liverpool', but what has it got to do with 'B' day?'

'The problem is we will be flooding the shops with vouchers and with so many going in on the same day they are bound to be spotted early so we need to delay that time as long as possible. A distraction is needed, get them looking for something else.

I understand "DD" was a dip, so he will have some hidden pockets. Is that right?'

'Yes', said "L".

'I suggest we put these counterfeit notes in one and leave him in such a way that he will come to the attention of DCS Chester. With a little prompting we can have the police and shop staff so worried looking for them in the tills they will pay less attention to the vouchers.'

'You really don't like Chester, do you?' said "M". 'You're setting him up.'

'Shall we vote gentlemen,' asked the "Professor". 'Those in favour please raise your hands?'

They all did.

Chapter 15

To say I was terrified at the thought of killing someone was an understatement, I was crapping myself. I couldn't kill a spider even when Helen was screaming the house down; I had to put them out the window. Now I had undertaken to do this; execute another human being. If I didn't go through with it the whole scheme would collapse and there would be a gang war between "Manchester" and "London"; and I would be lucky to end up in a wheelchair.

The "Professor" told me to be at his house at a certain time and date when the "Shadow" would phone and brief me; he also told me about the 'Shadow' and how they met.

'I will pick you up from the corner of George Street facing East at 0800 hrs tomorrow morning in a white transit van with a sliding side door,' said the Shadow. 'The door will have a cross inside a circle drawn on it. Do not look at the driver, it will be me; get in, close the door and sit down. There will be no windows, but a light will be on; it is better for all that you do not know where you are or who I am. When we reach the place where the execution is to take place I will stop, knock on the door; do not get out, is that clear?' When everything is ready, I will open the door and give you instructions; wear old clothes and gloves.

I cannot do this for you, but I can guide you. I will be with you throughout; do not do anything unless I have told you to do it. Do not think. Just do everything exactly as I say. Have a good breakfast not a fry up but something solid. You will not feel like eating but it is better if you have something in your stomach for the execution.'

There it was again that word 'Execution'; I truly felt sick.

'Thank you,' I said, 'what is your name?'

'You don't need to know my name or how to contact me. My anonymity is your safeguard no one can harm you unjustly without risking retribution from me. If you know who I am, you might tell them and then you and the "Professor" have no protection. If you cock this up or do not carry it through; I cannot protect you from the rule of the gangs otherwise the Professor and I would lose our credibility. It is the law of the criminal world and in their eyes justifiable.

If you must call me something, call me "Shadow".'

The weather matched my mood grey and sombre. I had picked on old pair of jeans, a tee-shirt, trainers and a warm jacket but I felt cold inside.

I was on the corner by 7:50 watching the oncoming traffic. Each vehicle had to stop in front of me at the junction then turn left into the one-way system. It was a busy time with everyone going to work. Car followed car then two buses each one stopping and waiting for a gap in the traffic to filter in. A white transit, I didn't look at the driver but went forward to open the side door when with shock I realised I had nearly got in the wrong van; there was no symbol on the door. I was now sweating, my nerves, the adrenaline starting to flow, I was twitchy.

Another white transit came into view, one of those oversize ones with a high roof, following more cars. I stared at the side door; there was something on it, but I couldn't see. As it came closer the symbol became clearer. It was chalked on the side. ⊗ As the van drew level with the corner it stopped; I slid open the door and got in, slamming it behind me. The van was full of old furniture, sofas and armchairs mainly; I fell back on one as it started forward and round the corner.

We drove for about an hour leaving the noise of the city behind, going over a cattle grid with its distinctive rumble. I could hear sheep then another cattle grid followed by a short stretch bouncing over a rough surface. The van stopped and the driver got out. The squealing of a large door being pushed aside was distinctive. The driver returned, the van moved forward, and the driver closed the large door. It was very quiet, then the knock on the side of the van to signify we had arrived.

I sat and I waited as instructed. It was nearly half an hour before the door slid open allowing me to see, not a man as I expected but the shape of a man with just a pair of fierce blue eyes.

He passed me a pile of clothing.

'Take your jacket off first then put these on,' he said, 'before you get out.'

There was a body suit made from some sort of thin woven paper/plastic material it had arms and legs with elastic cuffs and a hood.

'Those are over boots and that is a mop hat', he said.

Finally put on the mask and rubber gloves. I don't want us to leave any trace of our visit here and equally I don't want to take anything back with us on our clothing.

Now the subject is sitting in a chair; he is not tied because he is a vegetable. Hump's attack with the chair on his head did for him; you will be doing a mercy killing not an execution.

I've arranged for you to have a bolt. That's a sort of gun Vets use to put down horses. Instead of firing a bullet a steel rod or bolt shoots out killing the horse. The bolt is then pulled back into the gun on a spring. It's better than a gun as there is no bullet to match and convict you.'

He moved to one side, and I saw the figure in the middle of the barn, his head hanging forward with his hands between his legs.

'What is this place,' I asked?

'Don't worry about things like that. I told you not to think. Just do as I say.

The bolt is on the floor behind the subject. You place the barrel of the gun against the back of his neck, just below the skull and aim it up. The bolt will sever his cerebral cortex killing instantly; then retract leaving no evidence. Put everything back where you find it, that way nothing will be missed and left behind.'

The way he described it, he made it seem so clinical, so matter of fact.

Getting out of the van my legs felt like rubber, was I going to be able do this thing, kill someone?

I was glad I didn't have to look at his face as we approached from the rear.

'You're right-handed aren't you,' he said?

'Yes,' I replied.

'Stand slightly to the left of the subject'.

He picked up the bolt, placing it in my right hand. It was slightly bigger than a starter's pistol with a fatter barrel. Quite heavy for its size but fitted in my hand without feeling cumbersome.

'Now raise your arm and place it as I said. That's right. Now squeeze the trigger.'

I couldn't do it; I was freezing cold, but I was covered in sweat. I couldn't do it; he was a man like me but not like me, a thoroughly bad one but still a man.

'You must think of the subject as a 'thing' not a human being; a man loses that distinction when he rapes a girl, he becomes an animal and should be treated as one. Now he is a cabbage; just a vegetable, put this thing out of his misery; squeeze the trigger.'

I couldn't do it and started to shake.

'Don't think, just do it; squeeze the trigger, squeeze it, squeeze it NOW.'

I squeezed the trigger.

A sharp 'crack' sounded, and the bolt jerked in my hand violently, I nearly dropped it; the subject didn't move. I thought it hadn't worked but when I took it away from his neck, I saw the round hole where the bolt had done its work. My stomach heaved and my stomach contents rose into my mouth. I couldn't be sick as I was wearing the mask and had to swallow it again, it tasted awful. I wanted to run away.

'Well done,' said the voice in my ear, 'I knew you could do it. Now give me the bolt.

Go round to the front on the right and pick up the pair of garden secateurs and one of the small plastic bags.'

'What are these for,' I asked.

'We have to send the normal message to all the gangs you have done it.'

'What's that?'

'You have to cut off his fingers.'

'You're joking,' I exclaimed.

'No, I'm not. I'm very serious. Place a hand in a bag then using the secateurs cut off the little finger; think of it like trimming a twig off a rose bush. There will be little blood as the 'thing' is dead and the heart stopped.

Then take a new bag for each finger cutting off each one in turn, then the other hand. We need nine messages so you will have to cut off a thumb as well; you're lucky we only need one thumb as they're much harder to cut through.'

Lucky, I didn't feel lucky. I felt like I was in some sick nightmare. I went forward picked up a bag and the cutters and put the right-hand in. Opening the jaws of the secateurs I put them round the little finger and braced myself.

I couldn't do it. It was madness. I knew he was dead, but I couldn't do it, I squeezed. There was no sound just a soft crunching feeling. Releasing the grips the jaws opened but the finger did not drop in the bag; it just hung there by a piece of skin forcing me to do it again; I moved the jaws over and squeezed again. Finally, it came away and dropped.

I went on, a new bag a new finger, a new bag a new finger, then the other hand. Then the thumb; I had to open the jaws wider and when I squeezed it was much harder so holding the handles in both hands I squeezed until the jaws met with a sickening finality. I was finished. I didn't know I had been holding my breath but let it out in a big sigh.

'Now pick up the large bag.'

'What's that for'?

'You heard what Hump said he wants the part that attacked Rosie.'

'You mean'?

'You must cut off his dick.

I'll pull him back, so he is upright'.

As the figure sat up, his arms fell down each side, it was then I saw the figure didn't have any trousers.

'Now put it in the bag'.

I had to get down to the floor to slide it in.

'Take the knife that's on the floor; be very careful it's my filleting knife and very sharp. Don't cut down as it will bend away from you and you will have to hack it off. Put the knife under it, all the way over. Now pull the handle towards you, slicing upwards'.

There was little resistance to that knife and as the penis came away. It dropped to the bottom of the bag, the weight of it made it slip from my fingers to land on the floor with a smack that sounded like a wet fish.

Sitting on the door sill of the van, I asked, 'What's all the furniture for?'

'I stole the van last night from a couple of Cowboys who do house clearances. What they do is rip off all the good stuff and sell it; then the stuff they can't sell they take into the country and fly tip. This lot would have ended up in a hedge somewhere or in a farmer's field.'

'Won't they have reported it stolen and the police looking for it? You might get stopped.'

'The police won't stop me as I cloned some plates of a legitimate van. When I return it to their yard tonight and torch it, the furniture will make a great blaze. It will destroy any evidence we leave including all these coveralls. Now get inside and put yours in that plastic bag while I go and clear up and get the body ready for delivery.

'Delivery', I questioned?

'The parts you removed must be sent off and I will take the body down to London for Chief Superintendent Chester to fall over. I'll be back tonight and deliver the van back in the early hours. The cowboys can explain to the police why their 'stolen' van reappeared in their yard as a burnt-out wreck with false number plates.'

Chapter 16

Chester's day didn't start well; Mary, his wife, had finally had enough. She was fed up with everything being her fault, never his. It was her fault they had children. It was her fault they had no money. It was her fault they never had sex. He conveniently forgot that it was his insistence that she become pregnant and gave up her career in the force. She was a highflyer when they married; both Inspectors, with her on the Fast Track Scheme; she would have been earning twice as much as him by now. As for sex, he was always with those Toms, taking favours for not pulling them in; telling everyone else that he let them off in exchange for information. No wonder she didn't want anything to do with him.

Chester was the Detective Chief Superintendent of the Yard's Organised Crime Squad, and he was worried. He was on his way upstairs after being summoned to the office of the Chief Constable and he knew why.

Rumours and informants were his life blood. It was quite often the first hint that something was about to happen. He knew there was something in the air, his coppers' nose was twitching, and he had heard four seemingly unconnected things Joe, Boxing Day, Big and Nationwide. Then that corpse in the river turned up with those dodgy £10 and £20 notes followed by silence, which was worrying. He could find out nothing, the whole criminal society had closed ranks, his sources went dry.

Identification hadn't been straightforward, as the corpse didn't have any fingerprints. To be more accurate he didn't have any fingers; but whoever did this was not trying to hide his identity because they left a thumb, and his face was untouched. They were just making a point.

Perhaps it was the wedge of counterfeit bank notes in a secret pocket in the back of his jacket that made him call in at the mortuary that morning, maybe it was the lack of fingers, maybe it was an itch at the back of his neck he couldn't scratch.

It's called intuition and Chester had it even if he didn't have any scruples about fitting someone up. The autopsy had just been completed and the report available. Cause of death a penetrating wound to the back of the neck severing the cerebral cortex, killing instantly; luckily for the corpse the fingers were removed postmortem; an execution? An example? To whom was obvious but about what?

The corpse was a dip from one of the local London gangs. A particularly nasty gang and one with plans for expansion but that was all he knew.

The CC just pointed at the chair in front of his desk when Chester entered. His boss the DCC was leaning on the windowsill to the right of the desk.

'Keeping out of the firing line,' thought Chester; 'probably putting the whole sorry mess on Chester's plate.' Chester was not the only one who could sidestep trouble and give it to someone else.

'I've just come from the Home Secretary, following his meeting with the Prime Minister and the Chancellor of the Exchequer. It seems these counterfeit notes came from Africa. There are supposed to be billions of them left over from something in the Cold War everyone thought had been destroyed. The Prime Minister and the Chancellor are bricking themselves about those billions suddenly appearing. It would be a disaster for the government, so this is now a National Emergency in the making. MI5 wanted to take over, but the Home Secretary insists this is a Police matter as it involves British gangs; it has come down to me. 'The DCC is liaising with the other regions, but he says you are the expert; so, what's happening,' yelled the CC?

'I don't know. No one's talking,' said Chester.

'You don't know. Well, you had better bloody well find out and bloody quick. If these bank notes get circulated your head will be first to fall.'

Four months till Boxing Day, if no one was talking how the hell was he supposed to find out what was going to happen? He called in every marker he was owed, nothing. They wouldn't talk to him, or they knew nothing; at least that's what they said. There was an air of fear around; you could almost taste it.

Back at the Yard it was pandemonium in the Squad room. The gangs of Manchester's Moss Side had become united. This was unheard of and totally unexpected. Moss Side gangs were always at each other's throats. Inter gang feuds were commonplace, knifings and shootings the norm. To have them unite must have taken a very strong leader indeed and worrying for the police confirming their fears of a nationwide crime wave.

Chapter 17

'I've called this meeting at Joe's request,' said the Professor.

We were sitting once more in the lounge of the "Professor's" boat. All the members were there except Moss Side who was in the middle of a turf dispute. It seems that one street gang was selling drugs in a school in the next street. Knives had been used and worse threatened.

'We have two months until 'B' day and there has been a significant development,' I said. 'In the past I have said that the M&S voucher was too good to attack with any lookalike we could produce without the front-line troops getting arrested. This was true until last week. M&S have introduced an extra feature 'foil'. This is a shiny metal pattern that is put on with heat and a die. They haven't changed the printed design just added the new feature to increase security. On the table you will see the new design; the shiny foil is like the packaging on cigarettes and perfume.

I propose that as we have finished printing all the vouchers we intended and have a supply of paper left we print M&S vouchers. Not because we can print the design better but because the foil has been added. I think that many of the staff may see the foil and not look too closely at the printing or the watermark. Especially as they will; thanks to the Professor; be looking hard at banknotes. However, if we go ahead, I urge you to leave them to last as it is still the most likely place your people will be caught.'

'Can you print enough in time,' asked L.

'We can switch the night shift in all the print shops to the single design. The problem is the foiling. I don't know of any companies who would do it and we have no time to set one up.'

'I may have the answer to that,' said 'Liverpool'. 'I know of a foiling company who does those cigarette packets. I hold his marker for a very large gambling debt. He can work some of it off by doing the foiling we need.'

'If he says no, what do we do?'

'He won't and he will keep his mouth shut if he knows what's good for him.'

'So do we do it?' I asked.

'Shall we vote gentlemen?' asked the "Professor". 'Those in favour please raise your hands.'

They all did.

Chapter 18

One month till Boxing Day; the CC was vitriolic in his communications to Chester. It was made quite clear if he didn't come up with the answer, he would have great trouble getting a job as a School Crossing Attendant let alone in the police force.

He had only one option left, he had to contact his old boss ex ACC Gilmore. It was said he had contacts with the Criminal Underworld and was the one person who might know. Whether he would tell him was another matter as the "Professor" hated his guts ever since that matter with Chester's partner, another fast tracker who was sponsored by Gilmore. Back at the time he was in Manchester there was a kidnapping; Chester thought he could solve it himself and take the glory. He failed and a little girl died but Chester made sure his partner took the blame, and his partner hung himself in his garage a month later. But Chester was desperate, so he called, and they arranged to meet.

They met at the northbound service station on the M6 just south of Birmingham. It's anonymous but not wanting to risk a casual observer; the back of the Lorry Park was best. It's quiet at one in the morning as they parked between the trucks with their sleeping drivers; secluded.

Chester got in the Professor's car only to be met by a dense cloud of tobacco smoke. Getting straight out again he said, 'We'll sit in my car and leave that furnace behind'.

'Good morning Chester and what brings you out to such a lovely spot?' the Professor greeted.

'Not that pipe of yours. You should be prosecuted under the Clean Air Act', he said. 'It's about some other goings on, or what's about to. Rumours, somebody called Joe, Big, Boxing Day and it involves the gangs all over the country. Then this corpse turns up with no fingers. Apart from that I have no idea but I'm worried. Since that corpse there's been nothing and time is getting short. That's why I called you.'

'I've heard the same', said the Professor. 'When the body was found a message went out, 'keep your mouths shut' and that's what's happened. I'm not in the police anymore and I'm not a snout; I wouldn't last if I was.'

'I know all that, but this could become a National Emergency. No 10 is putting the pressure on for an answer. Look this is not common knowledge but when that body was found it had a wad of counterfeit bank notes in a hidden pocket. It seems they were printed by the Soviets during the cold war in some god forsaken African country. There were billions printed but something went wrong, and they should have been destroyed. The high ups are convinced they were horded by someone and are about to be circulated; the country will be in crisis; nobody will trust the money they have in their pockets. We must stop them.'

'Like you I've heard nothing since the message went out; I can't help you.

What do you know about this 'Joe' character,' asked the "Professor"?

'Nothing at all which is odd,' replied Chester, 'it just popped up one day from one of my snouts. It's so commonplace I am sure it's not his real one, just a code name. Whatever his name is he's got a lot of influence with the bosses if he's managed to get them to work together. That's the other worry from No 10; all the gangs working together; it would be like an army. Not even the police forces work together; how would they fight such an army? The whole country could be overwhelmed by an unstoppable crime wave.'

Chester fell silent after his outburst; it was as if he was just realising the scope of the nightmare he had just described. Outside the car the night was dark and silent. The lorries were like sleeping monsters just waiting to devour them like this monster threat was going to devour the country.

At last, the Professor spoke, 'Just think about what you do know.'

'Somebody called Joe,' said Chester.

'Dodgy £10 and £20 notes.

It's big.

It involves all the gangs.

It's happening on Boxing Day.

None of which helps.'

'What happens on Boxing Day?'

'Lots of things,' said Chester.

What do you do on Boxing Day?'

'I normally go to the races,' said Chester

'Does anything else happen on Boxing Day? What does your wife do?'

'The wife and daughter normally go to the 'Sales' at some big department store,' he said.

'Could that be another place they could pass lots of notes? Yes. That's it; a double hit the Races and the Sales.'

'I'll go straight to the CC,' said Chester, 'we'll have to cancel all the Christmas leave and flood the racecourses with plain clothes. This could be quite a feather in my cap.'

'More like early retirement,' the Professor thought.

Chapter 19

There were many disappointed race goers that Boxing Day morning as they couldn't hire a minibus anywhere. Every hire company had the same reason 'Sorry sir they've been booked up for months. I can hire you a coach or even a bus but nothing smaller.' It was the same story across the country, there was not a single minibus to be had anywhere.

It had been discussed at one of the meetings; using vans for moving the people around would look suspicious when they kept getting in the back with loads of carrier bags only to leave empty handed and return with more. It was agreed a minibus with passengers doing their shopping would be more 'normal' but to reduce the risk of questions they would keep on the move; never staying in the same place for long.

It was a great feat of logistics worthy of a military planner. Each store in every town in England, Scotland and Wales was visited and its location plotted on a map along with a note of how many tills. They also plotted places to park the minibuses while the 'shoppers' were 'shopping'. From over 2000 towns and cities the list was whittled down to just over a 1000 that had enough stores to make a concentrated hit worthwhile. Of these, fifty were cities in England, six in Scotland and four in Wales not counting St David's which was too small and the rest towns. The towns mainly had two buses going back and forth while the cities like Manchester had over 20. Each one would start at a different point around the city and weave its way from store to store. Dropping its load at a collection point and picking up more vouchers before crossing the city again, to another collection point near where they began. This was to be the pattern as they repeated their routes again and again. London was split into areas around concentrations of store locations and treated like small cities.

It was very cold in the minibus that morning, vapour coming from the mouths of the twelve passengers as they talked. The atmosphere was like an outing; everyone was excited although some were showing the effects of overindulgence on Christmas Day. The driver had stopped in a shoppers' car park in Salford and turned round to face them.

'Each one of you has an envelope with vouchers for a single store near here, so each of you will visit a different one. Some of you also have cash while those of you who are good at signatures have stolen credit cards. When we come back this way you will be given vouchers for other stores, so you won't visit the same store twice. Always buy items that are not in the sale and are more value than you have vouchers. Pay the extra either with the cash or credit cards. Don't worry if they start looking at the cash, they are looking for duds and all yours are genuine. Never buy anything for less than the vouchers as they will have to give you the change in new vouchers, and you don't want them to start comparing yours with new ones; you'll get collared if you do. Insist on a store carrier bag and put all the receipts and guarantees in the bag. We will be here until 9.30 so you must aim to be here no later than 9.25. Just get in the bus, hand over your bags to Bert and he will give you your next set of vouchers; we'll let you out at the next stop. If you are late, we will be at the next pickup point 100yds away in the road at the back of this store on the right and you will have lost your next lot of vouchers.

We will go on like this until we either run out of vouchers or you're all nicked; understand? Expect to have your collars felt sometime during the day. Don't forget you are innocent; you were duped by that person you bought the vouchers from on Christmas Eve in some pub or other. Be cooperative give them lots of information and descriptions but first ring your old mum to tell her what's happened and that you'll be late. You've all memorised the number?'

They all nodded.

'There are twenty other groups working in Manchester doing the same thing you are but if this is timed right you should be in different stores, but they may be some overlap. If you see someone you know, ignore them just get on with your purchases in the most inconspicuous way you can. Do not draw attention to yourselves; do not start talking to the cashier about your old mum sending you the vouchers. Just get in and get out. If you see anyone getting collared leave quietly and phone your old mum on the number and tell them just the facts, don't elaborate.

Next week you will receive in cash or cocaine or whatever you want the equivalent of 25% worth of everything you purchase. Do not try to fiddle us; we know exactly what we are giving you and we will know how much you spend. Don't forget we have the receipts. Anyone caught with light fingers will be dealt with severely and not paid.

It's now 8.30 the shops open at 9 so get in the queue with everyone else waiting for the doors to open.'

We sat drinking coffee a phone in front of each of us; the "Professor", "Manchester" and me, each with our own thoughts. "Manchester" had fortified the coffee with 'a dram to settle the nerves,' he said; then his phone rang. 'The first group has been dropped off,' he said.

There was nothing to say we just waited. The clock on the wall said 8:35.

'What's the first store,' I asked?

'They're starting with the department stores going for the big brands. Each group will have half an hour before the next group arrives and so on.

That way the faces keep changing so no single one gets remembered and picked out in the crowd', said "Manchester".

9:40 the phone in front of the "Professor" rang. 'Are you sure,' he said? 'We will just have to hang on till he phones in.'

'A couple in the first group at Harvey Nichols in Knightsbridge just got collared. 'L' has pulled all the rest out and moved to the next store.'

'I wasn't expecting any of the vouchers to be spotted this early,' I said. 'What could have gone wrong? Harvey Nicks must be heaving with shoppers, so how did they spot them?'

'We won't know for at least an hour. It will take the Police that long to get them back to the station, where he can make his phone call. We'll just have to hope it's something specific with Harvey Nicks and no one has talked so they're waiting for us,' said "Manchester".

John and Pauline had been together since they met in rehab. John had been an addict since his school days and Pauline from when she was a carer in an old peoples' home and stole their Tramadol tablets to get high. Christmas Eve had been very busy as they went from pub to pub using a list of pubs they had been given to visit. Whoever spotted a mark first started the story. Their mother had sent them £40 in gift vouchers for a new kettle but what they really needed was a fix. They then offered to sell the vouchers for £30 or even £20 if the mark was being stubborn. By the end of the night, they had over £1000 and promptly skimmed off £100 for themselves.

Luckily, they stashed the £100 before they went back to "London's" warehouse to hand in the nights takings for they were searched carefully for any misappropriated cash.

Boxing Day found them in the queue waiting for the doors of Harvey Nichols to open. They had been picked for Harvey Nicks because they looked respectable and fitted in well with the heaving mass of people, some of which had been camping there since the previous day for some special bargain or other. Finally, the doors opened, and the tide of shoppers flowed through the store; some grabbing designer clothes while others went for electrical goods at knock down prices. John knew what he wanted and went for a very nice watch while Pauline was in another part of the store purchasing designer handbags and shoes.

At 9.25 precisely they met just inside the entrance each loaded down with their purchases and went out together to board their bus only to be met by two burly security guards.

'Would you mind stepping back inside the store please,' they said.

The phones kept ringing for the next hour but no more arrests. The word was that it was pandemonium as the queues got longer as every bank note was checked. When vouchers were presented, they weren't even looking at them just stuffing them in the tills; it was working. However, schedules were not being kept to and 'shoppers' from different groups were arriving at the same stores at the same time.

Then the phone call we were dreading from 'L'. The "Professor" picked up the handset listening. Slowly he began to smile until it was a full grin, 'Stupid bitch,' he said, 'I trust you will deal with her later.'

'It was nothing to do with the vouchers,' he said. 'The girlfriend was picked up for shoplifting.'

The relief was tangible.

Bert was making his third drop of the day at the Piccadilly Station lockup when he saw the police car again. The first time it had been parked outside on the road opposite the entrance. Now it was right in parked across the yard opposite the lockup with a clear view of what was going in and out.

As soon as the outer doors were closed, he was out of the bus talking to 'Hump' who had taken over from Rosie.

'There's a patrol car outside watching us. Last time I came they were out on the main road; now they're just across the yard.'

'I'll talk to the boss.'

Boxing Day is usually quiet just cruising around in the police car; mainly looking for drunk drivers. That's what normally happens. People overindulge on Christmas Day then have a quick one on Boxing Day. They think they will be fit to drive but their body hasn't got rid of all the alcohol from the day before and them still over the limit. We had already picked up two drivers that shift and were parked on the road alongside Manchester Piccadilly Station. We were watching the traffic when a minibus full of people turned into the archway leading to the lockups under the station, which was most odd. Odd because we knew the units down there were closed for the holidays; it had been in the morning briefing.

'Keep an eye on the lockups. There won't be anyone working today and it'll be quiet, someone might take it into their head to break in one,' the sergeant had said.

It was even odder when the minibus re-emerged 15 minutes later with the same people; driving off the way it had come. Then another minibus repeated the sequence and another. It certainly warranted further investigation, so we drove in parking well over to one side to observe.

Twenty minutes later a minibus duly drove in and reversed up to a decrepit looking lockup when the pair of double doors opened and closed behind the bus.

Nothing happened for ten minutes then the small picket door opened, and a figure walked out to the main entrance carrying something bulky then returned shortly afterwards. Then another figure emerged and walked towards them. It passed near a light and the policeman in the passenger seat said, 'Relax its 'Hump'.'

When he picked up the phone and listened; "Manchester's" face went grey.

'Who are they?'

'I don't know. They're parked in the shadow across the yard; I can't see their faces. If they cotton on to what we're doing they'll radio in, and the place will be swarming with filth.'

'You forget there's no signal down there, they can't have reported in yet. Is there anyone in the other lockups today?'

'No one else is working down here today, it's deserted.'

'Hang on,' he said putting the phone down.

Manchester turned to the Professor and me saying, 'We made a mistake. We forgot that all the lockups would be closed today; there's no other traffic and the minibuses are standing out. Now there's a police patrol car parked across the yard watching everything.'

'We'll have to shut down that operation and divert everyone to the backup location,' said the Professor.

'It's not that easy,' replied Manchester.

'If they stop just one of those minibuses or search the lockup it will be all over. They'll report in and every minibus will be stopped and searched. When they know what's happening they'll call the other constabularies and the whole thing will crash about our ears. We will all end up behind bars.

Do you think "London" will forgive us if he finds out we could have stopped it? No, he will demand retribution. I wouldn't give a penny for our lives whether we are behind bars or not and don't think the Shadow will be able to stop him.'

'But there's nothing we can do,' I said. Do nothing and they will find out. Try and close down and they'll smell a rat and investigate.'

'We take them out before they can call it in and dispose of the car.'

'You're saying kill two policemen? I won't be party to murder,' I yelled.

'You're already a murderer; don't forget you topped DD.'

'Yes, but that was different, you know that. These are innocent policemen.'

'The law wouldn't see a difference and we can't afford your scruples; this is about survival.'

'This is my decision,' he said picking up the phone, 'but what do we do with the car?'

'Doesn't one of your legit companies sell fork-lift trucks?' asked the professor.

'Yes; why?'

'How do you deliver them?'

'We have a low loader with curtained sides and a ramp at the back.'

'Is there room for a car?'

'That's good thinking. It will be a bit of a squeeze, but it can take one.'

'Ok, here's what we do.'

'Picking up the phone again he said, 'Hump, take them out and leave the shooter in the car. It can't be traced but we can't use it again otherwise this will come back to haunt us.

Then close down the operation and divert the busses to the backup site. I'm sending the low-loader to pick up the car and take it to that disused quarry on Saddleworth Moor and it will be torched.

Go straight to the airport, mum will meet you there with your passport. Catch the first plane to Spain. Stay at the villa, I'll send Rosie out to be with you as soon as she's well enough to travel. We'll sort out some long-term arrangement for you later if necessary.'

'What did he say?'

'Close everything down and tell everyone to get ready to go home but first go to the entrance and put out the 'divert' sign.'

Bert went out of the picket door walking slowly to the entrance carrying a bright orange 'BT' warning fence. It had been stolen the week before just in case it was needed as an innocent looking warning sign round a manhole on the path outside. Now every driver making a drop would see it and automatically divert to the alternative lockup.

Hump walked to the back of the lockup to a solid brick wall out of sight of anyone. Making sure he wasn't observed he stood on a chair and felt along a ledge at the top. Finding the protrusion, he wanted he pushed it in until he heard a 'click' and a section of the wall swung slightly forward. Back on the floor Hump placed his fingers on the edge and pulled the false wall forward to reveal a cavity with shelves containing various boxes.

After putting on a pair of rubber gloves from a box on the centre shelf he lifted another down and un-wrapped the bundle from within to reveal a revolver and silencer. After checking the load, he tucked it in his jean's waistband at the small of his back covering it with his leather jacket.

When Hump got back to the entrance Bert had come back saying the sign was out and the police car was still there.

'Ok Bert,' Hump said. 'Get everyone on the bus ready to go but keep it inside till I get back.'

That walk from the small picket door to the patrol car was less than 100yds, but it was the longest Hump had ever taken. He didn't know what the Old Man was thinking, the Filth would never let this go but he hadn't been wrong before and prayed he wasn't wrong this time. Standing beside the driver's window he looked around making sure he was unobserved and tapped the glass. Bending slightly as the glass wound down his right hand behind him on the butt of the gun, he looked in the patrol car.

A pale blue light on the dashboard lit up their faces like two ghostly unrecognisable apparitions. Pulling the gun out he fired at the nearest face followed by a snapshot at the other. In the muzzle flash he recognised them, too late; they were on the payroll. The sound of those muffled shots echoed through the caverns like some death knell.

Both shots had found their marks. The first struck the driver in the eye as he looked up and the second in the middle of the forehead. They had both died instantly and unnecessarily.

With shaking hands Hump dropped the gun on the driver's seat and returned opening the big double doors so the bus could drive out. After closing and locking them he climbed into the front passenger seat, saying, 'Drop me up at the station I need to get a taxi.'

His mother was waiting for him at Manchester Airport, a small suitcase in one hand and his passport and ticket in the other.

'I've booked you a seat on the next flight leaving in half an hour,' she said sobbing. 'Let's pray you won't have to stay away.'

Then it was 12 noon and the phones went quiet; there was nothing to report; the hands on the clock slowly went round till just before 2pm when all three phones seemed to ring at once. Reports were coming in; people were being arrested. They had started passing M&S vouchers.

Chapter 20

The next day they just stood and stared. The cavern under Piccadilly Station was no longer stacked with boxes of vouchers; it was now stuffed to the roof with carrier bags.

There was a rainbow of colours and designs; from the orange of B&Q to the dark blue of Lakeland; containing everything from electric drills to food mixers.

'It will take us months, if not years to shift this lot and we have got ten more storage sites like this,' said "Manchester".

'Joe, you certainly made it work; I doubted at first that it would, but you proved me wrong.'

'The first task is to take as many as we can back for a refund,' said the "Professor".

'The shops will smell a rat,' said "Manchester".

'Yes, but they can't prove that it wasn't a legitimate sale so they will have to honour the receipt and as it was not for a 'Sale' item there is no reason for them to refuse. They may give vouchers in exchange, but they will be genuine. The rest you can sell off in the normal way except you should get more than you usually do having the receipts.'

That was how it panned out; nearly half were returned to the stores for refunds while the rest were sold off through the stolen goods black market at more than their usual prices. Most of the 'people' wanted their next fix rather than cash so the bosses made profit both ways.

The final total was just shy of £700 million that ended up as £500 million net. This gave the Professor and me £25 million each with the bosses taking the lions share.

The shortfall was because of M&S; they were just too good. Despite the silver foil and the threat of counterfeit bank notes being a distraction their staff still picked up the vouchers after only about half an hour. Then the call went out to every M&S store and people were apprehended. It was thought that about 30% of the people were caught in that single store chain before the rest disappeared.

It was nearly February and once more I was sitting with the professor in his study in front of a blazing wood fire.

'It's been five years since you met Agnes,' said the Professor, 'a lot has happened since then.'

'That's rather an understatement,' I said. 'I met Amanda, got divorced; became a criminal and a murderer.'

'Yes, but a very wealthy criminal, he said, 'and you made a lot of people very happy.'

Everyone was happy except me. I hadn't seen Amada for weeks; not since the scheme went live. She was always too busy to see me, off on some new venture for the Professor. When was it ending and our new life beginning? The details for the house on St Kitts had come through and the vendor had agreed to our price. The future looked wonderful; we had the house we wanted overlooking the bay. We could have each other and make love endlessly.

Then Amanda walked into the room and my heart sang and then faltered; she wasn't alone.

'Hi Joe', said Amanda, 'I'd like you to meet someone. This is Michael, my husband'.

I was devastated my mind and body felt numb. Then I realised what they had done to me.

'You're fucking lying bastards, all of you. And you Professor, like some puppet master pulling the strings at the centre of a web of lies and deceit, manipulating me. To what end, money?'

'I'm sorry Joe but it wasn't me who planned this, it was the girls. They cooked up this whole scheme when you were with Agnes in Lincoln. She pumped you for information about yourself and they decided the only way to get you to do what they wanted was a honey trap. You had to have an all-consuming reason to change your life and become a criminal. You were ripe to be turned. Your marriage had come to an end; your company failing.

Agnes told Amanda of your dreams and the perfect woman you always wanted; one that liked what you did, disliked what you did, making your sexual needs and desires come true. Amanda willingly became that living dream for a share in whatever we gained. We just didn't realise how significant a sum it would be, that was all down to you.'

'All those trips for the Professor they didn't exist; you were with your husband,' I shouted at Amanda. 'Those moments when we were together and you told me you loved me, all lies. All those times you made love to me it was just an act, the plans we made, more lies. Why? Why did you do it?' I asked.

'The money Joe, it was the money. As the Professor said he is sharing what he has made with Agnes and me; now Michael and I can live comfortably for the rest of our lives.'

My heart turned to stone. I wanted to shout and scream at her, it was unthinkable. This woman had stolen my heart while she schemed against me, used me, changed my life to suit her ends, now I wanted to kill her, but I did nothing; I just stood there, numb, staring at her until she left.

My life was in limbo; I couldn't quit from ConPrint as it might have raised questions, but I couldn't stay in this country with the money. If I started to spend it the police might be alerted and ask questions, so I had to carry on as if nothing had happened.

In the end it didn't matter the authorities denied everything; they were terrified of a copycat hit until the stores upgraded. Now you get a plastic card or just a till receipt with a barcode on. You no longer need the fancy voucher; a computer verifies everything as it happens so you can't fool it.

It's ironic but ConPrint was a great success, and many ex-prisoners were rehabilitated through the scheme and never re-offended. The Home Office copied the scheme setting up electrical, plumbing and building companies ConElec, ConPlumb and ConBrick. The government met its goal of going paperless with the demise of pension and child benefit books, MOT certificates, etc. It was just 14 years later than the target of 2000 with Car Tax discs finishing in 2014.

The police made a big thing about the killing of two policemen and their cremation in their car. It went on for months until someone talked and pointed the finger at Hump but for some reason the scam was never mentioned.

The police made it clear they wanted to interview Hump, but it never went any further than that, for the informer was never seen again; the rule of the jungle prevailed.

Just to be safe Hump stayed in Spain where he now lives with Rosie secure that Britain cannot extradite him as he hasn't committed a crime in Spain.

Aunt May died in the February of the following year and Aunt Jane, and I agreed to sell the company to our main competitor who thought he was cornering the market. Aunt Jane blossomed when she came out from her sister's shadow going on a world cruise where she met a widower and is no longer an old maid. I bought the house on St Kitts; I had nowhere else to go and moved in three years later.

I visited the whorehouse in the village from time to time, but I never made love again. Amanda had seen to that; I couldn't trust another woman enough to give my heart to. I had money to spare, lived in a wonderful place but I was alone and lonely; I had lost the woman I loved.

Not lost, for I never had her, I was a fool.

Chapter 21

An Alternative ending

A pale blue light on the dashboard lit up their faces and he recognised them; they were on the payroll. Letting go of the gun Hump tapped the side of his nose, 'Hi Lads. You haven't seen anything down here.'

The driver smiled as he put the car in gear ready to move off.

'I don't know what you mean Sir. It's so dark down here you can't see your hand in front of your face.'

It was nearly February and once more I was sitting with the professor in his study in front of a blazing wood fire.

'It's been five years since you met Agnes,' said the Professor, 'a lot has happened since then.'

'That's rather an understatement,' I said. 'I met Amanda, got divorced; became a criminal and a murderer.'

'Yes, but a very wealthy criminal', he said, 'and you made a lot of people very happy.'

Everyone was happy except me. I hadn't seen Amanda for weeks; not since the scheme went live. She was always too busy to see me, off on some new venture for the Professor. When was it ending and our new life beginning? The details for the house on St Kitts had come through and the vendor had agreed to our price. The future looked wonderful; we had the house we wanted overlooking the bay.

Then Amanda walked into the room and my heart sang as she ran into my arms.

'Darling,' she said in my ear, 'we are free and can be happy for the rest of our lives.'

We had a few holidays in the new house but didn't move to St Kitts for another three years. It took that long to wind everything up and move the funds offshore.

Agnes's Aunt 'Li' agreed to come with us and be our housekeeper. Soon after we moved to St Kitts, we learnt that it was Li who taught Agnes about sex, so it was only natural for her to continue by teaching us endless techniques of sexual bliss. At first it was most disconcerting to have her in the room with us saying do this or that but when she drove us to the heights of ecstasy, we forgot her presence.

Many years later I was sitting on the veranda with a visitor when we heard the front door open and a voice call, 'Joe, I'm home. Agnes's new granddaughter is lovely.'

Amanda had matured into an attractive slim grey-haired lady of great poise. Now in her early 70's she still walked with a grace that matched her figure.

'I'm sorry I didn't know you had company,' she said.

'This is Mr Adams darling he's an investigative journalist and I've been telling him the story about how we came to be here.'

'Good you've been going on about no one knowing what you and the Professor did and if they did, they wouldn't believe you. Now you have the opportunity, and I can have some peace. I'll make some tea,' she said turning and going back inside.

'Amanda got her wish about being an aunt. Agnes lives in the house you can see down there near the beach. It used to be the Professor's until he died last year. Agnes has two children and now her first grandchild.

'Why are you happy to talk about the scam?' asked Mr Adams, 'aren't you afraid of being arrested.'

'What would I be arrested for? A crime that was never committed. You haven't been able to find any record of one. Have you?

'No, I haven't, but there was that sudden dip in the economy at the end of '81 and all those rumours I have heard. It all came down to a name 'Joe'. You are the only 'Joe' that fitted the bill. You were in the right place at the right time. You had the knowledge. Then suddenly in '84 you come into money and moved here.'

'Who said crime doesn't pay?'

Please submit a review on Amazon and tell your 'friends' on social media about it.

If you have any comments or wish to tell me which ending you preferred; contact me at roy.adams.author@gmail.com .

Book 2 – The next generation

This will follow shortly. If you want me to put you on my mailing list, reply to the above email address.

Author's note:

At the time of writing in 2014 Sweden had built a large 'waste to energy' unit that is so effective the country has run out of waste to burn and now imports waste from Norway, sending back the ash for landfill.

Printed in Great Britain
by Amazon